JANIE'S
PRIVATE EYES

JANIE'S PRIVATE EYES

Zilpha Keatley Snyder

Delacorte Press

Published by
Delacorte Press
Bantam Doubleday Dell Publishing Group, Inc.
666 Fifth Avenue
New York, New York 10103

Library of Congress Cataloging in Publication
Data
Snyder, Zilpha Keatley.
    Janie's private eyes / Zilpha Keatley Snyder.
        p.   cm.
    Summary: Intent on investigating a rash of
dog disappearances, eight-year-old Janie forms a
detective agency and involves her friends and
unwilling family in tracing clues and suspects.
    ISBN 0-440-50123-7
    [1. Family life—Fiction.   2. Mystery and
detective stories.]
    I. Title.
    PZ7.S68522Jan   1989
    [Fic]—dc19   88-15480
                                              CIP
                                              AC

Manufactured in the United States of America

February 1989

10 9 8 7 6 5 4 3 2

BG

8/6/91

For everyone who wrote to me
asking for more Stanley stories

JANIE'S
PRIVATE EYES

Chapter 1

Afterward David more or less blamed himself. He should have realized that what Janie was up to could cause a lot of trouble. Not that he ever in the world could have predicted exactly what happened—not even a genius could have done that. But after the big New Year's Eve disaster it did occur to him that if he'd just paid more attention to the J. V. Stanley Agency he might have kept Dad and Molly's party from turning into the biggest wipeout of the Steven's Corners social season.

Molly and Dad hadn't had very many parties since they'd gotten married, and this one was supposed to be a really big bash. David first heard about it on a school morning early in December. He'd been on his way out to the bus stop and he just poked his head in the door of Molly's studio to tell her he was leaving. But the picture on the easel caught his eye, and he came on into the room to look at it. Molly, David's stepmother, was standing in the middle of the room with her hands on her hips. She was staring at the picture too.

It was cold in the studio, and Molly was wearing her winter painting outfit: Levi's with leg warmers, an old paint-smeared field jacket of Dad's, and ratty old gloves with the fingers cut out. Her long hair was tied back with a strip of canvas to keep it out of the paint. For a person her age, Molly tended to be kind of relaxed about appearances, particularly her own, and particularly when she was painting.

The picture on the easel was of two blurry figures, one of which looked vaguely like a very large animal and the other more or less resembling a very small human being. David looked from Molly to the largest blur on the canvas and then back again.

"Nightmare?" he asked.

"Umm!" Molly nodded. "And Blair."

Blair was David's six-year-old brother, and Nightmare was Blair's dog. Actually, Nightmare, an enormous Irish wolfhound, belonged to the whole Stanley family, because Dad said that nobody the size of Blair could possibly own that much dog all by himself. But that didn't change the fact that Nightmare obviously thought he belonged to Blair. Or else maybe the other way around.

"It hasn't been easy getting them to pose," Molly said. "They either wiggle constantly or go to sleep."

"Yeah," David said. "I can imagine. Well, anyway I think the picture is . . ." The thing was, the painting did look kind of—well, out of focus, maybe, but that probably wouldn't be a good way to put it. Molly was sensitive about her paintings, especially since she'd started her blurry period. Molly's pictures used to be the kind that looked quite a bit like what she was painting, but since she'd gotten into blurriness, they didn't. Or else they looked like whatever it was she was painting, in a very deep fog.

Molly sighed. Then she took the picture down off the easel and leaned it against the wall. Face backward.

"Aren't you going to finish it?" David asked.

She untied the canvas ribbon, shook her hair loose, and hung the ribbon over the top of the easel. "Not now. I think I need to let the concept mature for a while. And besides, I'm not going to have much time for painting in the near future. Not with Christmas coming, and then the big party."

David knew about Christmas. Did he ever! In a family with five kids Christmas was not something you forgot about. But he hadn't heard anything about a party. "What party?" he said, and Molly told him all about it.

It was, she said, going to be a really big event. Molly and Jeffrey, David's father, were planning to invite not only their old friends from the university but also all the new ones they'd made recently in Steven's Corners.

"We've met so many nice people lately," she said, "particularly since our debut on Channel Forty." She smiled at David and patted his shoulder. "Thanks to our family hero."

David winced. Molly was referring to the fact that he, along with Blair and Nightmare, had become local celebrities by capturing some escaped criminals. The capture and all the newspaper and television stuff about it had happened back in November, but it still made

David uncomfortable to be reminded of his own performance on the local TV news program. The problem was that the television cameras had given him a nearly fatal case of stage fright. But the rest of what had happened—the being suddenly famous in the whole community, as well as at home and school—had been okay. He grinned at Molly.

"Blair and Nightmare did as much as I did," he said, trying to look modest.

"No. Not really," Molly said. "And it's true about meeting people. We'd hardly met any local people before your remarkable exploit shot us all into the limelight. I think that Steven's Corners old-timers tend to be a little suspicious of newcomers. And when they heard we'd bought the Westerly house . . . you know. Outsiders buying a place that had been a local landmark for years and years: there may have been a bit of resentment. But that's all changed now. People have gone out of their way to be friendly lately. And Jeff and I have been thinking that it would be fun to introduce some of our new friends to the Wheelers and the Bradleys and a couple other of our favorite people from the university."

At the time, David had thought the party was a really good idea, and he hadn't changed his mind even after Molly mentioned that she'd invited Mr. Prentice and Ms. Baldwin. Mr. Prentice was the principal of Wilson Junior High, and Ms. Baldwin taught eighth grade math and was David's homeroom teacher. If Molly had asked him he might have said that he didn't think that Ms. Baldwin was exactly the party type. But since she didn't ask, he didn't say anything. It didn't make that much difference to him one way or the other.

But it did seem to make a difference to Amanda, Molly's fourteen-year-old daughter, and, of course, David's stepsister. A lot of things made a big difference to Amanda, and Molly's guest list seemed to be one of them. David and Amanda were out in front of the house waiting for the school bus when he started talking about the party. It got her attention right away. She stopped practicing a new dance step up and down the edge of the blacktop and began to ask questions.

So David told her what Molly had said. He was kind of enjoying telling about it because he was usually the last kid in the family to pick up on interesting rumors, and this time he seemed to have heard something first. Amanda listened quietly until he got to the part about the guest list.

"Get real!" she said. "They didn't ask old Betsy B. to the party, did they?" Amanda was in ninth grade at Stevens High now, but when she was still at Wilson Junior High she had been in Betsy Baldwin's math class. "And Prentice, too? You've gotta be kidding! I can't stand it." She clutched her forehead and staggered around as if she were about to pass out.

"Why not?" David asked. "Prentice is okay, and so's Ms. Baldwin—at least, most of the time."

Amanda looked at David as if he were an idiot. It wasn't easy to say exactly what Amanda did with her face to make you feel like an idiot, but whatever it was, she was good at it.

"But they're teachers!" she screeched. "Can you

imagine partying it up with teachers? I mean, as if they were human or something."

David thought about it. "But Dad's a teacher," he said. "And he's great at parties. You said so yourself once. Remember?"

For a moment Amanda looked confused. "Yeah," she said in a puzzled tone of voice. But then she shrugged and grinned. "He's a college professor. That's the difference, I guess."

In a way, David wanted to ask what difference she was talking about, but in another way, he didn't. The whole thing sounded like good argument material, and arguments with Amanda tended to be long and noisy. And the bus was due any moment. Unless David felt like letting half the bus in on a discussion of teachers and whether or not they were human, it seemed like a good idea to cool the whole thing. So he did.

Of course, the little kids thought the party idea was great when they found out about it that evening. Janie and the twins had been lying on their stomachs in the middle of the floor when David came into the living room. Janie had been reading out loud. When David told them what Molly had said they all three acted like it was the best news they'd heard all year.

The six-year-old twins, Blair and Esther, obviously liked parties just because they liked people, and Janie— well, Janie liked excitement. The more the better. And a big party at the Stanleys' must have looked to her like better excitement material than usual, even though it was going to be a strictly adult event. At least, that's what David supposed was behind her wild enthusiasm —at the time.

"Wowee!" Janie shouted. "Really, David? Wowee! Great!" And then she jumped up and started bouncing around on the tips of her toes, the way she always did when she was excited.

"When?" she said between bounces. "How many people? Who's coming? Oh boy! Oh boy!"

Blair sat up quickly and moved back out of danger, and Nightmare, who had been sprawled on his side not far from Blair, got up and moved too. He'd been bounced on before when Janie got excited, and he knew enough to get out of the way. But Esther, who'd always had a stubborn streak, stayed where she was, yelling, "Watch out, Janie. Watch out! You're going to step on me!" and then a minute later, "OUCH! You did! You did it, you dummy. You stepped right on me."

Esther sat up and rubbed her ribs. The she started kicking with both feet in the general direction of Janie. David sighed. Janie and Esther tended to get into more physical disagreements than anybody else in the family. Esther started scooting toward Janie on her rear end, still kicking, and Janie stopped bouncing and stepped back out of reach.

"I didn't step on you," she said. "That was just your sweater."

"It was skin, too. It hurt!"

"Well it wouldn't have been skin if you weren't so fat," Janie said. "There wouldn't have been skin away out there if you didn't eat so much."

Esther jumped up and began to swing at Janie with both hands. "I'm not. I'm not fat. Daaa-vid! Make Janie say I'm not fat."

"Basta!" David yelled, grabbing Janie with one hand

and Esther with the other and holding them apart. *Basta,* a useful word that the Stanleys had picked up during their year in Italy, means "enough." Dad used it sometimes when David and Amanda were quarreling, and David himself used it a lot around Janie and the twins.

After he'd yelled *"Basta!"* a couple more times, Esther began to cool down and all three of the kids began asking questions about the party.

"Will it be a snack party or a whole big dinner party?" Esther asked.

David grinned. Esther's question was what Dad called a Typical Tesserism. "Tesser" was Esther's nickname, and a "Tesserism" was any comment that had to do with her special interests. Besides eating, the thing that mattered to Esther was for everybody to do exactly what they were supposed to, exactly when they were supposed to do it. So Tesserisms were any kind of remark that had to do with law and order, or food.

As soon as David admitted that he hadn't thought to ask about the menu yet, Esther ran off yelling, "I'm going to ask Molly. I'm going to ask her what there'll be to eat at the party."

Blair, who never had a great deal to say, had just one question, and that was whether Nightmare was going to be invited.

"Sure," David said. "He'll have to be invited. He's been real good about meeting new people lately. And besides, everyone will want to see him. Some of the people who'll be here haven't had a chance to see him before."

But if the twins' questions were typical ones, Janie's were pretty weird, even for her.

After Esther had gone to look for Molly, Janie scooted up on the couch beside David and sat there for a while, swinging her legs and looking thoughtful. Janie was very small for her age, which was eight, and when she sat on most chairs and couches, her feet didn't touch the ground. So she swung her legs and puckered up her face for a while and then started asking some really ridiculous things. Like if any of the women who would be at the party were going to be beautiful and mysterious.

"Beautiful and mysterious?" David said, laughing. "I doubt it. Peggy Wheeler's not too bad-looking, and neither is Molly, for that matter. But I wouldn't call either of them mysterious."

"Hmm," Janie said. "How about people with . . . records."

"Records? What kind of records? Molly said there was going to be music, but I think they'll use Dad's tape deck mostly."

Janie looked disgusted. "Not that kind of records. I meant police records. People who have, you know"— Janie raised her eyebrows and rolled her eyes suggestively—"shady pasts."

"Wow!" David said. "You must be kidding. College professors and people from Steven's Corners? With shady pasts? Stop dreaming, kid."

He started out of the room, still chuckling, and stumbled over Janie's book. It was an old book with a dusty green cover and no jacket, probably from the collection of books that Molly had inherited from her uncle.

David picked it up and looked at the title. It was *The Maltese Falcon.*

"Give it here," Janie said. "I'm reading it. To the twins."

"To the twins? This book? Janie! This isn't a kid's book."

"That's all right," Janie said. "I explain it to them a little as we go along."

"Oh yeah?" David said. "How do they like it?"

Janie shrugged. "Pretty much. But not as much as they liked *The Hound of the Baskervilles.* They liked the part about the hound."

David grinned. "Yeah," he said, "they would." Actually, he hadn't read *The Hound of the Baskervilles,* but Blair and Esther had always liked dog stories.

At the time, David didn't think any more about Janie's choice of reading material. Of course, a stranger might have wondered about an eight-year-old reading an adult mystery story, and translating it into something a couple of six-year-olds could understand. But having known Janie for so long, David didn't give it another thought. Perhaps he should have, but he didn't.

Chapter 2

Christmas was great that year. Of course, Christmas is always great for little kids, but David had developed a theory about there being a certain age at which a Christmas slump sets in. The slump tends to happen the year you suddenly become too old for toys. You know you're too old for toys and you don't really want them, but when you suddenly don't get any it's a shock.

For David that had happened the year he was eleven. That had been the first Christmas after Molly and Amanda joined the Stanley family. He could still remember how let down he'd felt. On the afternoon of that Christmas Day he'd been glooming around in the kitchen, smelling the turkey and trying to feel enthusiastic about eating Christmas dinner, when all of a sudden Molly had given him a sympathetic smile.

"I always get the Christmas afternoon blues," she told him. "The excitement is all over and all that's left is

11

the mess. But there *is* one thing you can be thankful for."

"What's that?" David had asked.

"You can be thankful—*ouch!*" Molly said. She threw down the knife she'd been peeling potatoes with and stuck her finger in her mouth. Then she sat down at the kitchen table beside David, and sucked her finger. After a minute she took it out of her mouth and waved it in his face. "See what I mean," she said. "You can be thankful you don't have to cook Christmas dinner."

David looked around the messy kitchen and nodded. "Yeah. I see what you mean," he said. After that he sat down at the kitchen table and shelled some peas and he and Molly made up a song called "The So Long, Santa, Blues."

But that had been two years ago, and some things had changed since then, and some hadn't. Molly still wasn't much of a cook, but at least Christmas was back to normal. This time when he opened his presents, David got the same jolt out of a state-of-the-art tape recorder and a new backpack and a really great Guess jacket that he used to get out of kid stuff like games and construction sets and remote-control robots.

The tape recorder in particular was just what he'd been hoping for. He'd been wanting one for a long time: ever since September, when he'd finally made a firm decision about his future career.

Up until that time he'd wavered between planning to be a geologist, because Dad was one, or a veterinarian, because he liked animals, or else a psychiatric social worker, because, as he once told Amanda, growing up in the same family with both a Janie and an Amanda was as good as taking an advanced course in abnormal psychology.

Amanda had slugged him harder than usual, but that wasn't the only reason he'd given up on being a psychologist. The real reason he'd changed his mind was that he suddenly discovered his writing talent and decided on a career as an author. And according to Mr. Edmonds, who was a writer himself as well as being the best English teacher at Wilson Junior High, every writer needs a tape recorder.

As David had mentioned several times to Dad and Molly, there are all kinds of ways a writer can use a really small tape recorder. You can, of course, keep it handy in your pocket or by your bed at night to record good ideas for stories or articles. You can even record stuff while you're traveling or waiting in train stations or airports, and then type it up later, when you get home. And if you are going to be a newspaper reporter, which David was seriously considering, you absolutely have to have a tape recorder to record interviews with famous people and that kind of thing. Apparently, mentioning it had paid off, because the Sony recorder in its professional-looking carrying case was exactly what he'd been hoping for.

The rest of the family got the usual for their respective ages and sexes and personalities. Amanda got clothes and some tapes of new wave music, plus some cash from her father, like always. Amanda's father always sent her wads of cash for birthdays and Christmas. For Esther there was a doll and kid-size kitchen stuff. And the present Blair liked most was a fancy new brass-studded collar.

Actually the collar was for Nightmare, of course, but for weeks and weeks when anyone asked Blair what he wanted for Christmas it was the only thing he ever mentioned, except that now and then he also asked for dog food. Like when David took him to see the Santa Claus in Macy's, and right there on Santa's lap in front of the cute teenage girls who were being Santa's helpers, he said that all he wanted for Christmas was a dog collar and a bag of kibble. Which left Santa kind of speechless and gave a couple of his elves fits of hysterics. But that was what Blair wanted and that was what he got—a brass-studded dog collar and a lot of kibble, plus a few other things like games and books.

Janie got the really complicated and expensive chemistry set that she'd been dropping megaton-size hints about for quite a while. She'd apparently found it listed in a catalogue that Dad brought home from the university. The stuff in the catalogue was supposed to be for high school and college students, but nobody worried that Janie wouldn't be smart enough to handle it. No one had ever worried about Janie not being smart enough for anything. With Janie there were plenty of things to worry about, but that wasn't one of them.

The fact was, however, that she had never shown any particular interest in chemistry before. David could recall when she'd gone through spells of being a Shakespearean actress, a gossip columnist, a detective, and a vampire, but she'd never shown any signs of being a scientific type before. Not even a mad scientist, although there you were getting close. The chemistry set was an important clue, of course, but if David thought about it at the time he just supposed it was another one of Janie's crazy projects and let it go at that.

As it turned out the chemistry set was one tip-off that David could have picked up on, and there had been another small sign that Janie was up to something—an actual sign, on a piece of cardboard taped to the outside of an old briefcase Janie sometimes played with. What it said was THE J. V. STANLEY AGENCY, INCORPORATED, PRIVATE EYES. Actually he did ask about the sign. At least, he remembered making some kind of wisecrack about it, like asking if she kept her private eyes in the briefcase, because he'd like to rent a pair. "I'm tired of blue eyes," he'd said. "I'd like to rent a pair of brown ones, private or otherwise." Janie had ignored him, and he hadn't thought any more about it.

There had been one other event that David might have followed through on. That had been something that happened at the shopping center in Steven's Corners a few days before Christmas. It was a Saturday afternoon, and he'd gone in on the bus to finish his Christmas shopping. He'd been at the Wagon Wheel Mall for quite a while, and he'd made his last purchase and was heading for the bus stop when something strange caught his eye.

The Wagon Wheel Mall had a rustic farmyard kind of motif, and there were these boardwalks between some of the buildings, with split-rail fences on each side. David was just passing the walk between the stationery store and the Mexican restaurant when he noticed something rustling around in the deep ground cover that grew between the fence and the next building. The first thing that came to his mind was *rats,* which gave him a crawly feeling on the back of his neck. Stopping dead in his tracks he whispered something like "Ugh!" and backed up a step or two to get a better look.

That was when he noticed that the ivy was wiggling all the way down to the corner as if a whole army of rats, or whatever, was on the move. He was backing away when the first wiggle rounded a camelia bush and something lifted its head—which was blond and curly and strangely familiar. The rat in the ground cover was Janie Stanley, and right behind her was Esther and then Blair and a couple of other little kids.

"Janie?" David said. Janie's eyes got big and she made a gasping noise and dived back out of sight around the camelia. There were a few frantic whispers and a couple of seconds later the whole string of little kids was crawling back the way they'd come. This time Janie was in the rear. David marched down the boardwalk, stepped over the low fence, and pulled her out of the ivy by the back of her jacket.

"Janie Stanley," he said, giving her a slight shake, "what do you think you're doing?"

"Hi, David," Janie said, with her most innocent smile. "Are you Christmas shopping? We're Christmas shopping too. Aren't we, Esther?"

Esther had crawled out of the ivy and was trying to climb over the fence. "Christmas shopping?" she said, and then, "Oh yes. Yes, we're Christmas shopping, David."

David couldn't help grinning. Esther had always been a lousy liar.

Janie turned to look down the alley, where there was still a lot of activity among the ground cover.

"It's okay," she called. "Come on back, Blair. Come on, Thuy. It's only David."

Blair came out from behind a bush then, followed by two other little kids. The others were a girl about Janie's size and a boy who was even smaller. A lot smaller, as a matter of fact. David had seen the girl before. She was in Janie's class at school and she'd come over to the Stanleys' house to play a couple of times recently. She was Vietnamese, and her name was pronounced something like Thwee, and she and Janie seemed to get along really well. Thuy was about the same height as Janie, which meant they were probably the two smallest kids in the third grade. They looked kind of neat together, as if they'd just escaped from somebody's doll collection.

The other little kid was obviously Thuy's little brother. He was about as big as nothing, with the kind of face that on a one-to-ten cuteness scale would be at least an eleven. He looked about as dangerous as a baby rabbit, but when David gave Janie another little shake, he threw himself on David's ankle and bit it.

Actually he only got pants leg, but it took both Janie and Thuy to pull him loose, and for the next minute or so, while Janie held on to him and Thuy lectured him in Vietnamese, he kept showing his sharp little baby teeth and rolling his shiny black eyes toward David's ankle. But the lecture seemed to work, because by the time it was over he had calmed down, and when the girls let him go he marched over to David and held out his hand.

"Huy is sorry," Janie said.

"Who is?" David asked.

"Huy. That's his name. He thought you were trying to hurt me. He wants to be friends now."

"Oh yeah?" David stuck out his hand, bending way over so as to keep his ankles back out of reach. "How you doing, man?" But the little kid didn't attack again. He just shook David's hand firmly and then marched back to stand beside his sister.

"I mean it," David said. "I want to know what you guys are up to, and how you got downtown."

"Dad brought us," Janie said. "Dad brought us down to Christmas shop. Didn't he tell you?"

David remembered then that Dad had taken Janie and the twins into town that morning, but he'd supposed that they'd all gone home long ago. He knew Dad had returned, because he'd been in the kitchen talking to Molly just before David left to catch the bus. So how did the kids get back downtown, and what in the world were they doing crawling through the landscaping at the Wagon Wheel Mall?

He never did find out, really. Janie kept insisting they were Christmas shopping, and Esther went on backing up her story. And Blair went on saying nothing, which was standard operating procedure for Blair. Thuy and Huy didn't talk either, but David didn't try to make them, since he supposed they didn't know much English.

The next Westerly Road bus was about due, so David herded the Stanley kids down to the bus stop, and Thuy and Huy went off on their own. He'd given up asking questions for the time being, but when he got home he did ask Dad a few. Dad was working in his study, and when David came in he put down his pen and swiveled his chair around.

"I hear you found the kids and brought them home just in time to keep Molly from forming a posse," he said.

"Yeah," David said. "I guess they were downtown quite a while."

According to Dad the little kids had gotten a ride into town with him when he went in to buy some new lights for the Christmas tree. But when he was ready to go home, they weren't, and Janie had talked him into letting them stay to finish their shopping and then come home on the bus.

"She gave me a sob story," Dad said, "about how long it takes to shop when you have to be so careful about money because of having such a small allowance." He grinned at David, and David grinned back and raised his eyebrows. There was a family joke about how much Janie loved money and how she was always scheming to get a bigger allowance, or part of someone else's. "They certainly stayed a long time. Molly was beginning to worry. Were they still shopping when you found them?"

"Wellll . . ." David said. He didn't really want to rat on the little kids, and besides, he couldn't think of any believable way to explain what they had actually been doing when he found them.

"Yes?" Dad asked.

"Well, that's what they said they were doing." And then to change the subject he added, "They were with

Janie's Vietnamese friend. You know, Thuy, or whatever her name is, and Huy; that's her little brother."

"I've met Thuy," Dad said. "Cute kid. And smart as a whip too. Understand they've only been in this country a few months and she's already speaking an awful lot of English."

"She is?" David said, surprised. She certainly hadn't spoken any to him.

Dad nodded. "Mmm. I was talking to her the other day when she was here playing with Janie. Her father has a job at the nursery. Hope they're going to be happy in Steven's Corners. Seems as if they might be a bit lonely. I don't believe we have any other Vietnamese families in the area. It must be hard for them."

So then Dad got wound up about the problems of all the different waves of refugees that had come to America since way back in the early days, and David pulled up a chair and sat down. Being a college professor and all, Dad tended to get wound up now and then, and when he did you might just as well get comfortable. Actually, the waves-of-refugees lecture turned out to be pretty interesting, but it kept David from doing any more thinking about what Janie might have been up to, and by the next day he'd forgotten all about it.

Chapter 3

On December 31, the day of the party, the whole family pitched in to get everything ready. In the morning everyone cleaned house—*all* morning. Cleaning the old Westerly house was at least an all-morning job.

The problem wasn't the house itself, even though it was big and old and a little bit decrepit. The problem was that except for Esther, who was too little to make much difference, no one in the Stanley family had any natural interest in housework. So in between occasional all-out clean-up projects, things tended to get pretty funky. The projects, or "cleaning frenzies" as Dad called them, usually only occurred when company was coming—or else when Dad started threatening to carry his machete around with him so he could chop his way back to civilization if he got lost in the debris.

As usual the cleanup project began with everyone cleaning his or her own room. And as usual Dad brought a garbage pail up to the top of the stairs to hold all the cleaned-out junk. It was a big garbage pail, but one full-fledged Stanley cleaning frenzy could fill it right up. According to Dad, the debris from a Stanley housecleaning could be analyzed the way archeologists do the different layers under ancient cities.

"This would appear to be an Amanda layer," Dad said, peering into the garbage pail. "Fashion magazines, fast-food cartons, half used lipsticks, and unfinished homework." Dad dug a little deeper to where he began to come across the stuff from David and Blair's room. Because of Nightmare and Rolor, the crow, and all Blair's other pets, the Blair-David stratum looked pretty awful and smelled like a pet shop.

"Ancient dusty dog kibble," Dad said, poking around gingerly with one finger, "and, let's see . . . hamster pellets, well-chewed bones, apple cores, something that looks like petrified liverwurst, breadcrusts, feathers, and a few other objects best left unmentioned. But mostly dog hair. Lots of dog hair."

"Tell me about it," David said. "I'm probably going to have to sue, like the coal miners with black lung. Only I'll have fuzzy lung from so much dog hair and crow feathers."

Dad laughed.

"Or crow hair and dog feathers, as the case may be," David added, and Dad laughed some more. So did David, although he tried not to. He was working at not laughing at his own jokes. "And what about the Janie and Esther layer?" he asked Dad. "What kind of artifacts does a Janie-Esther civilization leave behind?"

"Well, that one's more difficult to classify," Dad said,

digging a little deeper. "Everything from old coloring books to what seems to be half a crystal ball. What I see here is a deep cultural split. Judging by its artifacts, I would say that this was a civilization on the verge of civil war."

"You can say that again," David said. "Did you hear Janie yelling a little while ago? She'd mixed up some kind of special powder with her chemistry set, and while she was looking for something to keep it in, Esther vacuumed it all up. I got there just in time to prevent bloodshed."

"Well that's what she gets for doing experiments on cleaning day," Dad said. "What was she working on?"

"I don't know. She didn't say."

Janie hadn't said. But there might have been a clue in something Esther said—or yelled, rather. While Janie was still trying to slug her and she was backed up in the corner defending herself with the vacuum cleaner wand, Esther was shouting something about there not being any fingerprints. "It looked like plain old dust to me," she yelled, and then a lot of other stuff too. But the vacuum was making so much noise that David didn't catch all of it.

When the upstairs rooms were all done, the whole family went to work on the downstairs. But even with everyone helping they didn't finish until midafternoon. Then the three little kids went off to an early New Year's Eve party that some mother "with more courage than common sense," Molly said, was giving for kids who were too young to stay up until midnight. While the little kids were gone, Molly and Amanda worked on the party food, and David helped Dad fix the loud-speaker system.

Ordinarily Dad listened to his stereo in his study, but for the party he'd rigged up some speakers downstairs in the living room and dining room. The wires had to be run down through the stairwell and along the ceiling of the downstairs hall and on into the two main party rooms. When they were through stapling the wires in place, Dad took David up to his study and showed him the tapes he wanted played during the party.

David was to be in charge of music for the evening. Most of the tapes Dad had picked out were show tunes and light classical pieces, except for a stack of big band stuff that had been popular in the days when people like the Bradleys were young. Bill Bradley was the head of Dad's department at the university, and a little bit on the elderly side. David was to wait to play the big band tapes until late in the evening, when, according to Dad, everyone would be feeling sentimental and nostalgic.

"Not to mention smashed?" David said, and Dad grinned and said, "Well, perhaps a bit of that too. But not yours truly. I'm not planning to indulge. Might have to provide transportation for some guests who need a ride home."

When the wiring was done, Dad and David joined Molly and Amanda in the kitchen and helped spread tuna goop on little tiny sandwiches and stuff cheese spread into celery sticks. By the time all the trays and dishes of food were put away in the refrigerator, the little kids had come home, and there were only a couple of hours until the guests would start arriving. David went up to his room, which was so neat he hardly recognized it, except that all Blair's little furred and feathered friends were still there, running around in their clean cages, wondering what had happened to all their familiar piles of junk. David symphatized with Blob, the hamster, for a while, and then he crashed on the window seat and didn't wake up until Amanda stuck her head in the door.

"You better get ready," she yelled. "It's almost time for the Big Event."

The first ones to arrive were Steven's Corners people, like Mr. Prentice, the principal at Wilson, and Ms. Baldwin, David's math teacher. Ms. Baldwin looked so different David did a kind of double take before he realized who it was. In the classroom she usually wore dull-colored skirts and sweaters and no makeup, but tonight she was wearing huge dangly earrings and a dress made of slinky-looking green material, with a matching vest-shaped thing covered with shiny green fringes. Actually, David preferred the skirts and sweaters, but Amanda seemed to be impressed.

"Did you see Betsy?" she whispered to David in the hall. "She's really styling. Wonder where she got that fringy thing. I could go for that."

The next couple to show up was the Dorfmans. David recognized Mr. Dorfman, who was the president of the bank in Steven's Corners, but he hadn't met Mrs. Dorfman before. It turned out that she was plump and talkative. Or as Amanda put it, loud and fat.

"Did you see that one?" Amanda said, when she and David happened to run into each other at the downstairs coat closet. David was hanging up the Prentices' coats and Amanda was carrying a huge shaggy fur.

"What one?" David asked.

"That loud fat one that was wearing this dead grizzly bear or whatever it is. Did you hear what she said to me?" Amanda made her voice sound like it was coming out of her nose. "Well, well, you must be the stepsister. Quite the young lady, aren't we!" Amanda held up the fur coat and glared at it. "Aren't *we*!" she said. "Can you believe it?"

David laughed. "What did you say?"

Amanda shrugged. "Nothing—at least, not out loud. Under my breath I said, 'Quite the old fat one, aren't we.'"

On his way back to get some more coats it occurred to David that Amanda really had lightened up recently. In the old days she would definitely have said it out loud.

Next came a bunch of university people whom David had known for years, like Bill Bradley and his wife Janice and George and Peggy Wheeler. That was only the beginning, but after that David went up to Dad's study to start the music, so he didn't see most of the other people arrive.

On his way upstairs he met Janie and Blair and Esther on their way down. They were tiptoeing in single file, with Janie in the lead, and they all three were so shiny and slicked down it was funny. Blair's curls were just beginning to pop up from where they'd been flattened by a wet comb, and Esther's round cheeks looked like they'd been polished. And Janie—well, more than anything else, Janie looked excited. More excited than you'd expect, maybe, for just being allowed to spend a couple of hours at a party for grown-ups.

"Well, well," David said. "Look at the party people. You dudes going to swing a little?"

"We get to stay up until ten," Janie said. "Dad said so."

"And we get to have some refreshments," Esther said.

"Where's Nightmare?" David asked Blair. "I thought he got to come to the party too."

"Later. Dad said later." Blair's big eyes were even bigger than usual. "Dad said he'd tell me when."

"Well, let me know when you're going to get him," David said. "I want to see what he does—and what everybody does when they see him. I'll bet some of them are going to think they've had a few too many."

He started on up the stairs but Blair grabbed his arm. "Too many what?" he asked.

"Come on." Janie started pulling Blair downstairs by his shirt. "Come on, I'll explain it. David meant people will think Nightmare is like what you see when you drink too much. Don't you remember? I told you once, about pink elephants."

Blair looked puzzled. "Nightmare isn't pink," he said.

David leaned over the railing, trying to hear the rest of the conversation, but he didn't catch any more and the kids disappeared into the dining room. He was grinning as he went on into Dad's study and put on the first tape.

The rest of the evening David dropped in on the party now and then, but most of the time he spent in the study reading a good book and changing the tapes. He liked it fine that way. He got to see what was going on and eat some party food without having to hang around making conversation with a lot of adults all evening. Around nine o'clock Blair peeked into the room and said he was going to get Nightmare, so David went down to watch. That was something he didn't want to miss.

Because Nightmare had been mistreated by his first owner he'd been nervous around strangers when he first belonged to the Stanleys, particularly if the strangers were adults. He'd pretty much gotten over that now, but still David wondered how he was going to react to all those people.

Nightmare did start to growl a little when he and Blair got to the living room door, but after Blair whispered to him for a minute he calmed down and started wagging his tail. Then somebody looked up and saw him and made a gasping noise and everything got very quiet.

"Great Caesar's ghost!" George Wheeler said to Blair, "What is that thing, Blair? Is it as dangerous as it looks?"

Blair shook his head. "It's our dog," he said in his soft breathy voice. "It's Nightmare. He likes people now."

George laughed. "Blair says his large friend here likes people," he announced to the whole room. "I'm hoping he means socially, not as an after-dinner snack."

Everyone laughed and Nightmare ducked his head and looked embarrassed, as he always did when you laughed at him, and everyone started crowding around him, laughing and talking. Before long he was stretched out in his favorite spot in the middle of the floor and a bunch of people were sitting around him scratching his stomach. David watched for a while and then went back upstairs.

He was still reading and playing tapes a little later when Amanda came in. She had one of her Duran Duran tapes and she wanted David to play it.

"Okay," David said, "but if there's trouble, remember—it wasn't my idea."

Amanda was grinning a fairly fiendish smile as she shoved the tape into the deck. "Trouble?" she said. "Why should there be trouble?"

When the music, if that's what you wanted to call it, started, David and Amanda went out and sat on the stairs to see what people would do, but except for a few wisecracks, no one seemed to pay much attention. Amanda was disappointed.

"Nobody even complained," she said disgustedly. "They must be drunk or something." She took her tape out of the stereo and went off to bed.

Some time after ten David heard Janie and Esther and Blair going past on their way to bed. He started the big band stuff then, and when it was finished he dozed off, just waking up in time to put on the last tape, which was "Auld Lang Syne," and rush downstairs to watch everyone blowing on paper horns and kissing each other. Nobody seemed to be at the pink elephant stage, but Mrs. Dorfman was having some kind of an argument with Mrs. Prentice, and George Wheeler finished kissing all the ladies and started over again. David found a relatively quiet corner on Molly's little love seat behind the bamboo plant and settled down to watch.

By one o'clock a few of the guests had gone home, but most of them were still in the living room, packed onto all the chairs and footstools and even sitting on the floor. Ben Haley, who taught music at the university, was playing a bunch of old songs on the piano, and everyone was singing. David was about to go on up to bed when all of a sudden he realized that Ben had stopped playing and that a strange loud noise was coming out of the speakers that Dad had rigged up.

The speakers sizzled for moment and then the sizzle turned into a voice, a loud witchy-sounding voice that was saying, "And did you see that tacky green dress with the fringed vest? Makes her look like a Christmas tree."

The voice stopped and the sizzling noise started up again. David peeked around the potted bamboo. Everyone was looking toward the couch by the fireplace, where Ms. Baldwin was sitting in her green and fringy outfit.

The sizzle turned into a different voice, too soft to hear clearly, and then the screechy one cut back in. "And that dreadful animal. Why anyone would want to expose their guests to a dangerous beast like that, I can't imagine. And the food! All those soggy little sandwiches and runny dips. You'd think Professor Stanley would hire a caterer if his wife can't do any better than—"

The high-pitched voice broke off suddenly. In the living room everyone was looking in a new direction. David got out from behind the bamboo and moved to where he could see what they were looking at. It was Mrs. Dorfman. She had gotten up off Molly's rocking chair and was standing with her hands on her hips glaring around the room. "Well! I never!" she said in her high screechy voice. "I've never been so insulted in all my life. Elmer! Get my coat. We're leaving."

It was very quiet in the living room as the Dorfmans headed for the hall. Except for Dad, who jumped up and followed them out, nobody moved or spoke. From the hall there was the sound of Dad and both Dorfmans all talking at once, and then the slam of the front door. Dad came back into the room. Everyone was looking at him. He shook his head with a bewildered expression on his face. "Don't ask me," he said. "I can't explain it. Unless our famous poltergeist has returned."

Then Molly giggled and said, "Anyone for another soggy sandwich?" and everyone roared with laughter.

"I'll have a couple," Peggy Wheeler said. "And as for you, Nightmare, you great dangerous beast, come over here and give me a kiss."

Everyone laughed some more, and then Ms. Baldwin jumped up and went over to the Christmas tree and took a red glass ball off it and hung it on one of her fringes. Then she kind of tiptoed in a circle and everyone practically fell on the floor laughing. Everyone except Dad, that is.

Dad was looking around the room, and all of a sudden his eyes lit on David.

"David?" he said, frowning.

David shook his head frantically. "Not me," he said. "I can't explain it either. It came out of the speakers, that's for sure, but I was down here. I've been right here since I put on 'Auld Lang Syne.' I didn't . . ."

He stopped and for a minute both he and Dad stared up toward the study, and a moment later they were running up the stairs.

In the study the stereo was still on, but the tape slot was empty. A tape was lying on the floor. As Dad picked it up David saw that it was "Auld Lang Syne." Dad was turning it over and over in his hands, staring at it, when something made David turn around. The door to the study was creaking open.

Questions with words like *poltergeist* in them were flitting around in David's mind, and the hair on the back of his neck had started to prickle, when a round blue eye appeared in the crack.

"Oh! Oh!" a small voice said, and the eye disappeared.

David dived for the door, pushed it open, and grabbed a fleeing figure by the back of its pajamas.

It was Janie, of course.

Chapter 4

"Oh hi, David," Janie said when David grabbed her by the back of her pajamas. "What did it say? Could you hear what the tape said?" and she went right on chattering as he pulled her backward into Dad's study. "I couldn't hear it up here. The sound was only coming out downstairs. Could you hear it? What did it say, David?" Then she saw Dad and changed her tune. "I didn't mean to, Daddy. I forgot about those new speakers. I didn't know it was going to come out down there."

Dad's face was wearing its dangerous deadly calm expression. David couldn't help feeling a little sorry for Janie—and more than a little glad *he* wasn't the guilty party this time.

"Jane Victoria," Dad said. "What have you been up to?"

Janie clasped her hands in front of her chest, as she always did when she was getting ready to be dramatic.

"I didn't mean to," she said again. "Really I didn't! Cross my heart and hope to die. I poked the same buttons as always when we play our tapes on your stereo. I thought the sound would only come out here, in the study. I just wanted to hear it better. It wasn't loud enough on David's recorder."

"My recorder?" David was frowning. "What were you doing with my tape recorder?"

"We just borrowed it," Janie said. "We didn't hurt it. We just borrowed it to record some evidence."

"We?" Dad said. "You mean you weren't the only one involved?" He turned toward David.

"Not me," David said quickly. "I told you, I don't know anything about it. Whatever they've been doing, I wasn't in on it."

"The twins," Janie said. "The twins and me."

"And I," Dad said. "The twins and I." With Dad you got grammar lessons with everything, even the third degree. "And what do you mean by 'evidence'?"

Janie stopped clasping her hands and began balancing on her tiptoes, the way she always did when she was revved up about something. Her eyes widened and her voice got shivery with excitement.

"We were getting evidence," she said, "on a murderer. We borrowed David's tape recorder and we put it in the bamboo plant by the love seat. You know, like where people might go to whisper secret things to each other, like about crimes and things. But the twins wouldn't stay awake to sneak down to get it, so I had to do it alone. And then when I listened to it there wasn't anything but faraway noises, except this one part that was almost loud enough to understand. So I brought it in here and turned the stereo up high."

"You certainly did," Dad said. He was still frowning, but David suddenly realized that he was having a hard time trying to keep from laughing. "So you planted a bug in the bamboo to catch a murderer and all you got was Grace Dorfman insulting Ms. Baldwin's taste in clothing and Molly's cooking."

"Grace—Mrs. Dorfman?" Janie said. "Was that who it was? I couldn't tell." Then her eyes narrowed. "What did she say? Did she say anything about . . . Mr. Rupert?"

David looked at Dad and Dad looked back with a kind of questioning expression, as if he expected David to explain it. David lifted his shoulders and shook his head. "Don't ask me," he said.

"Mr. Rupert?" Dad said to Janie. "Why should she say anything about Mr. Rupert."

Mr. and Mrs. Rupert owned Rupert's Groceries in the old part of Steven's Corners. They had become good friends of Dad and Molly's and probably would have come to their party if they hadn't gone to Hawaii over the holidays.

"Why would she be talking about the Ruperts?" David asked. "They weren't here."

"I know that," Janie said. "I didn't mean that Mr. Rupert, anyway. I meant the old one."

"Alvin Rupert senior?" Dad asked. "But he's dead."

"I know." Janie went up even higher on her toes. "Dead." She came down and leaned way forward and lowered her voice to a whisper. *"Murdered."*

"Jeff!" It was Molly calling from the foot of the stairs. "Jeff. People are leaving. Are you coming down?"

Dad hurried to the door and called, "Be right there." He turned back to Janie. "I've got to go explain—and apologize—to our guests. But I'll be back to hear the rest of this. I'm sure you're wrong about Al's father, Janie." He went on out the door, shaking his head and muttering "Murdered?" under his breath.

"David," Janie said as soon as Dad had gone. "What did Mrs. Dorfman say? David!"

David was still busy thinking about murder and old Mr. Rupert. Grandpa Rupert, as most of the kids in town called him, had died a few weeks before; around Thanksgiving, if David remembered correctly. For a while afterward everyone talked about him a lot. They talked about him mostly because everyone missed him. He had been a real nice old guy, who used to give away free candy if you came into the store when he was tending it for his son and daughter-in-law. But the other reason the kids all talked about Grandpa Rupert's death was because he'd died of a heart attack in the park. For a week or two people kept talking about it and showing each other which bench he'd been sitting on when it happened. But nobody had said anything about murder. At least, not that David had heard.

"DAVID!" Janie said again. "What did Mrs. Dorfman say about Grandpa Rupert?"

"What?" David said. "What are you talking about? She didn't say anything about Mr. Rupert. She just said that Ms. Baldwin looked like a Christmas tree and that Molly's sandwiches were soggy. Oh yeah, and that Nightmare was a dangerous beast."

"Really?" Janie looked disappointed. "Are you sure that's all she said?

"Janie," David said, "what makes you think Grandpa Rupert was murdered?"

"Well . . ." Janie had gone up on her toes again, but now she came down flat-footed and held up three fingers. She folded down one of them and said, "First of all, there's a motive."

"A motive? You mean somebody had a reason to kill Grandpa Rupert?"

Janie narrowed her eyes and nodded slowly.

"What motive? Who would want to kill a nice old man like that?"

"Well, how about Al and Geraldine?"

David stared at Janie in horror. "His own family? Why would they do a thing like that?"

"For his money. In detective stories people always get killed for their money. Or for their property, like the grocery store. So they could inherit it."

"That's ridiculous," David said. Janie was still holding up two fingers. "What are those other two for? I hope they make more sense than the first one."

Janie looked at her fingers. "Two is that there wasn't any autopsy. When people die mysteriously there's supposed to be an autopsy. You know, an operation to find out what he died of."

"I know what an autopsy is," David said. "And how do you know there wasn't one?"

"Because I asked Dr. Cox."

"Well I don't suppose they thought there needed to be one. Geraldine told Molly that Grandpa had heart trouble for years."

Janie shrugged. "Okay, but wait till you hear number three. Number three is that we have a witness."

"A witness? You mean somebody saw the—the murder?"

"Well, not exactly the murder. But somebody saw a man talking to Grandpa just a few minutes before, and then that somebody went down the slide, and stood in line for a while to go back up, and when he got to the top again it had already happened."

"Holy cow!" David said. "A kid. Your witness was a kid. Who was it?"

Janie looked at David suspiciously. "Well, don't tell, because we're keeping it a secret until we get some more proof. But the witness is a member of the J. V. Stanley Agency." Janie smiled and nodded slowly and then, as if she liked the sound, she said it over again: "The J. V. Stanley Agency, Private Investigators. Incorporated. Don't forget the 'Incorporated.'"

"J.V." David asked, and then it dawned on him. "For Jane Victoria."

Janie nodded proudly.

"The Jane Victoria Detective Agency." David grinned. "Okay. I get it." So that was it, he was thinking. Janie and the twins had decided they were some kind of Sam Spade types, and they'd been going around looking for a crime to investigate. They'd probably been . . . "Hey, wait a minute," he said. "Was that what you were doing that day at the shopping center? You know, when I found you guys crawling around in the landscaping?"

Janie frowned and stuck out her chin. "We were tailing the suspect, and then just when he was about to do something suspicious, you had to come along and spoil it."

"The suspect?"

Janie nodded. "That's right. Mr. Garwood, the mailman. You know, the tall one with a bald head. He was the one that our witness saw talking to Grandpa just before it happened. We'd been tailing him for a long time and he was mostly just pretending to deliver the mail, but after a while he started acting kind of nervous and suspicious and then—"

"No wonder he was acting nervous," David said, "with a gang of little nerds following him around all afternoon. That'd make anybody nervous. And why do you think he was just pretending to deliver the mail? That's what a mailman is supposed to do, isn't it? And who was this witness anyway, the one who saw him talking to Grandpa Rupert?"

"Huy. It was Huy," Janie said.

"Who-ee?" David said. "What do you mean, who-ee?" But then it dawned on him. She was talking about the Vietnamese kid. "Oh, you mean that little girl you've been friends with lately?"

"No. Not Thuy. Her name is Thuy. I mean her little brother."

When David realized she meant the peanut-size ankle biter he nearly cracked up. "You're kidding," he said. "You mean your witness is a two-year-old who can't even talk yet? Some witness."

"Huy is four," Janie said. "And he talks a lot—in Vietnamese. He talks to Thuy and she tells us what he says. Huy was in the park with Thuy on the day Grandpa Rupert died, and he was playing on the slide and he could see the bench where Grandpa was sitting from the top of the slide. And he saw that mailman talking to Grandpa just before the murder."

"Murder again?" Dad asked as he came in the door. "What is all this about a murder?"

Janie sighed. "Do you want to tell him?" she asked David. "I'm tired." She rubbed her eyes with both fists, mugged an unbelievably long and complicated yawn, and went all limp and droopy-eyed. "I'm going to bed."

But Dad grabbed her around the middle and sat her down on the edge of his desk. "No you don't, Miss Thespian," he said. "You're going to recover from your sudden attack of exhaustion long enough to tell me what's been going on, and you'll sit right there until you do."

Dad meant it. Jeffrey A. Stanley usually meant what he said, and nobody except Janie ever seemed to doubt it. But this time even Janie was convinced. She looked at Dad for a minute and then sat up straight and knocked off the droopy-eyed bit. "Okay," she said brightly. "It's very exciting. We've started our own detective agency, and—"

"You've what?" Dad said.

So then Janie went over the whole thing again: how she and the twins and Thuy and Huy were investigating the supposed murder of Grandpa Rupert, and how their main suspect was Mr. Garwood, the mailman. This time she added some parts she hadn't told David, like how they'd gotten Mr. Garwood's fingerprints off the steering wheel of his mail truck.

"I was getting the fingerprints while the suspect was taking a break in Rosie's Coffee Shop, and I sent the rest of the agents into the shop to make sure he didn't come back too soon. All except Blair, who stood in the door to warn me when the suspect was about to leave. So then Blair did, and I wasn't finished, so I had to tell Blair" — Janie put her hands around her mouth and whispered, —" *'Emergency Delaying Action, plan one,'* and so they did plan one and it worked fine."

"What was plan one?" David asked.

"Plan one was for Huy to tip over the suspect's mailbag and spill out all the letters."

"Wow!" David said. "How come the littlest guy had to do the dirty work?"

"That's exactly why!" Janie sounded like a teacher praising a good student's answer. "Huy's too little to blame. And besides, he's the bravest. Huy will do anything."

David nodded. That he could believe: anything— even biting innocent people on the ankles.

"Janie," Dad said. "About the fingerprints. How did—"

"With my crime kit," Janie said, "from the chemistry set."

"Your chemistry set?"

"Yes. Didn't you read about it in the catalogue?" Janie narrowed her eyes and begin to recite, " 'Including a complete for-rens-kick—' "

"Forensic," Dad interrupted.

"That's what I said: forensic. 'Including a complete forensic chemistry kit. Materials and instructions for taking fingerprints, typing hair and blood, and performing other investigative techniques.' Didn't you read that part, Daddy?"

Dad shook his head ruefully. "I read it, looking for anything dangerous, like poisons or explosives. But not carefully enough, I see. Go on. Janie, let's hear the rest."

He kind of collapsed into his leather chair and Janie went on—and on, and on—and when she had finished Dad sighed and covered his face with his hand for a minute. Then he took it away and said, "Well, Janie, that is all very interesting and, I must say, impressive. It seems to me that the J. V. Stanley Agency has achieved a great deal, considering the short time it's been in business, as well as the relative inexperience of its operators."

Janie beamed.

"When you think," Dad went on, "that in a very short period of time you've succeeded in shocking all our guests, offending the Dorfmans, hurting Ms. Baldwin's and Molly's feelings, and probably giving a poor innocent mailman a nervous breakdown, it's impressive to say the least. But I'm really afraid, Janie, that the Stanley family and quite possibly the whole community is less in need of investigations and more in need of peace and quiet. So *no more* detective agency. Do you understand me, Jane Victoria? The J. V. Stanley Agency—"

"Incorporated," Janie said in a small voice.

"Incorporated," Dad said. "The J. V. Stanley Agency, Incorporated, is hereby declared out of business. Finished. Bankrupt. Kaput!"

"Daddy," Janie began, sounding as if she was about to cry. "Daddy, please. Couldn't we at least finish the cases we're working on?"

"Like the Grandpa Rupert murder," Dad said.

"Janie, you know as well as I do that Grandpa Rupert wasn't murdered."

"No, no. Not that one. I don't care about that one anymore. But we've just started on another one, and it's terribly important and—"

"Another murder?" Dad asked.

"Well," Janie said, "it might be. So far Phoebe's just missing, but she may have been murdered."

"Phoebe?" Dad asked.

"Phoebe Ferris," Janie said.

Dad looked puzzled. "Who is Phoebe Ferris?"

All of sudden it dawned on David. "Dad," he said, grinning, "I think I know. Phoebe is Mrs. Ferris's poodle. I heard about it at school. Mrs. Ferris has been at all the schools asking the kids if anyone's seen her dog."

"I see," Dad said. He lifted Janie down to the floor and started out of the room. At the door he turned and looked back. "No!" he said. "No more murder investigations. Poodle or otherwise."

Chapter 5

When David came downstairs the next morning the kitchen was empty, but Amanda showed up while he was eating his cereal. She came into the room droopy-eyed and grumpy, as she usually was before she'd had her breakfast. But she woke up in a hurry as soon as he started telling her about Janie's murder investigation and what it had done to the New Year's party. In fact, he couldn't remember ever seeing Amanda laugh quite that hard before.

She made David tell parts of it over two or three times, and every time she laughed harder. She was still laughing so much when she started getting stuff out of the refrigerator that she slopped the milk, and she went on having occasional convulsions while she mopped up the spill with a paper towel. Then she kind of collapsed against the refrigerator door and just sat there, gasping and giggling.

David was laughing, too, but every once in a while he managed to say, "Shh! You'll wake everybody up."

Leaning against the refrigerator, Amanda gasped, "Ms. B. the Christmas tree," and then, "Soggy sandwiches and runny dips. Oh man! I'll bet Mom loved that." She staggered to her feet, threw the paper towel away, and flopped into the chair next to David, still grinning. All of a sudden she reached out and grabbed him by the front of his shirt.

"You nerd," she said, holding her fist up in front of his face. "Why didn't you wake me up? I miss out on everything around here. I ought to punch you one."

"Hey, wait a minute," David said in between a couple of leftover blurps of laughter. He knew she didn't really mean it about punching him. Not that she wouldn't do such a thing, because she had before and probably would again if she were really mad. But at the moment she was actually grinning and frowning at the same time, and that meant she wasn't too serious. "Cut it out," he said, grinning back. "I couldn't tell you. It all happened too quickly and—"

He stopped suddenly and listened. An unmistakable sound, a little like a bunch of tin cans rolling down hill in a garbage can, was coming from the direction of the driveway. Amanda turned him loose and went to the window.

"Garvey?" David asked, scooping up the last couple of bites of cornflakes.

Amanda nodded. "Mmm. What does he think he's doing, coming here so early on New Year's Day?"

David got up, put his bowl in the sink, and joined

Amanda at the window. "The same thing he's always doing. Trying to make time with his girlfriend. Ouch!"

Amanda's elbow had hit him in the ribs. "Girlfriend!" she said. "I'm not his girlfriend, and you know it"

"I know it," David said, "and you know it, but I don't think Garvey knows it."

As a matter of fact, Pete Garvey, who was almost fifteen even though he was still in the eighth grade, had been in love with Amanda ever since last fall, when she'd punched him in the nose for trying to beat up on David. Before that he'd been following David around for weeks trying to punch, staple, and mutilate him, but since he'd found love he'd reformed, and now he only followed David around trying to be his best friend. Actually, having Garvey as a best friend was almost as embarrassing as having him for an enemy—but a lot safer, so David didn't complain. At least, not very loudly.

Out in the driveway Pete was rattling to a stop on his little old rickety bike. Amanda and David watched as he climbed off it, leaned it against the fence, and started down the path to the porch. Pete was the tallest and biggest kid in David's class, with muscles on top of his muscles and a way of moving that always made you think of a grizzly bear getting ready to charge. When Pete lumbered up onto the back porch Amanda went back to the table and sat down.

"Aren't you going let him in?" David asked.

"Who, me?" Amanda said. "Are you kidding? Let him in yourself."

When David opened the back door Garvey just stood there for a minute, almost splitting his broad face with a chipped-toothed grin. "Hi Stanley," he said. "Happy New Year, and all that . . ." Looking over David's shoulder he saw Amanda and stopped, gulped, and then went on. "Stuff," he said. "All that stuff. Hi, Amanda."

Amanda slowly chewed a mouthful of cornflakes before she said, "Hi yourself, Garvey. What's with you?"

Pete just stood there staring for a minute before he pulled himself together. "With me?" he mumbled. "With me? Oh. Oh, yeah. I come to see Stanley about working on a reporting thing together for Mr. Edmonds's class." He turned to David. "You thought about it yet, Stanley?"

David nodded. "Yeah." He'd thought about it all right. The journalism project had started before vacation, and right at the beginning Mr. Edmonds had explained that the final was going to be a team effort, with two people collaborating on researching, writing, and photographing a news item of local interest. And right from the first David had had a sinking feeling that Garvey was going to ask to be his partner. And sure enough, just before vacation, Garvey had asked. David had said he'd think about it.

"Yeah, I thought about it," David said. What he had thought was that Garvey would be about as useful on a newswriting project as a surfboard in the Sahara Desert, but what he said was, "Sure, Garvey. Why not? Got any good ideas yet?"

"Ideas?" Garvey mumbled, but David could see he wasn't paying attention. Garvey's attention span tended to be on the short side. "What's that stuff?" he was saying. "Is it any good?"

Garvey was pointing at the box of Corn Crunchies. "It's okay," David said, and then went on to ask, "Want to try some?" even though he already knew what the answer would be. Where food was concerned, Pete Garvey's answer was always the same.

"Sure," he said, plopping himself down at the table and reaching for a bowl. "Why not?"

So Garvey ate Corn Crunchies, and David had another bowl to keep him company, and Amanda started telling Garvey about the mess Janie had made of the party the night before. He grinned a few times but he was too busy eating to say much. In fact, he seemed to be concentrating so hard on the cornflakes that David wasn't even sure he'd been listening, but when Amanda finished he said, "Yeah, that Janie is some kid. She's been into that detective stuff for a long time, huh."

"Well, she was for a while last fall," David said. "Before the convicts got caught." He was too modest, of course, to mention who'd caught them. "She was going around playing detective for a while, but after that was over she just stopped talking about it. I thought she'd gotten discouraged because she didn't get to solve anything about the convicts. Boy, that was dumb of me. If I hadn't thought she'd given up on being a private eye I might have guessed what she was up to before she sabotaged Molly's party."

"Given up?" Amanda said. "Janie? Get real! That one never gives up."

"Right," David said. "I guess all she did was go underground."

"Who did? Who went underground?" a voice said,

and there was Janie herself, coming in the door. She was still wearing her pink romper-suit pajamas, and her curly hair was hanging all around her face in little blond corkscrews. She was looking particularly cute, dumb, and innocent, which was usually a bad sign.

David grinned. *"You* went underground," he said. "You quit talking about being a detective and everybody thought you'd gotten over the idea."

"I know," Janie said. "That's exactly what I did; I went underground. Wasn't that smart of me? See, the thing is, when people know there's a detective around it puts them on their guard."

"Personally," Amanda said, "what puts me on my guard is knowing there's a disaster machine named Janie Stanley around. Man! Did you ever make a mess of Mom and Jeff's party, Shrimp."

Janie looked indignant. "No I didn't. I didn't make a mess of the whole party. The only part that got messed up was a little tiny bit right at the very end."

"Yeah, well from what David said I guess Jeff and Mom didn't think it was such a little tiny bit. According to David your dad told you that your dectective agency was out of business. Isn't that right?"

Janie's angry frown turned into a worried one, and she sighed deeply. "I know," she said. "And it's just terrible. Because we'd just gotten started on a very important case, and now we can't go on with our investigations."

David grinned. "You mean the case of the missing poodle?" he asked and then before Janie could answer he started explaining it to Amanda and Pete. "It's about

Phoebe, old Mrs. Ferris's poodle. She's disappeared or something."

"Yeah, I heard about that," Amanda said. "Some old lady came to the high school and talked to the student body about her poor missing dog. She was really bummed out about it."

"But that's not all," Janie said eagerly. "Phoebe isn't the first one. There were two or three others before that, and now everyone's blaming the Trans."

"The whos?" Amanda asked.

"Thuy and Huy's family," Janie said. "This kid in our class named Billy Boggs has been going around saying the Trans stole his dog, and probably Phoebe and the others too. And a lot of people believe it."

That seemed to get to Pete, who up until then had seemed to be too busy scarfing Corn Crunchies to pay much attention. "What's that?" he said with his mouth full of cornflakes. "That Chinese bunch stole a mutt? Why would they do that?"

Janie looked at Pete and sighed. "They didn't," she said in a patient tone of voice. "In the first place, they're not Chinese. They're Vietnamese. And they're *not* stealing dogs, either. It's just that that stupid Billy's been saying that they did. I don't know why. Billy says lots of dumb things."

"Maybe it's true," Amanda said. "How do you know they didn't?"

"Because Thuy says they didn't, and Thuy never says anything that isn't true. But people are blaming them anyhow, and Thuy is so worried. She says that Mr. Wright who owns the nursery came over last week and told her father that he was thinking of selling the nursery again."

"Again?" David asked. "Did he sell it before?"

"No. He just thought about it before, when he retired from running it. But then he decided to hire the Trans to run it instead. But now he's thinking of selling it again, and Mr. Tran thinks it's because he's heard the rumors about the Trans being dognappers. And now I can't solve who really did it and it's just terrible." Janie came over to David's chair and leaned on his shoulder. "Don't you think it's just terrible, David?" she said, staring into his eyes and smiling a sad pitiful smile.

He knew better of course, but for just a moment he felt kind of sorry for her. Then he came to his senses and said, "Janie, what are you trying to lay on me this time?"

Janie looked shocked and offended. "I'm not laying anything on you, David. It's just that you are my only big brother, and I just thought maybe you could help save the Tran family from going to prison for dognapping, because you're always so good at investigating and everything and—"

"Man oh man! What a snow job," Amanda said.

Janie went around the table and leaned on the arm of Amanda's chair and put her hand on Amanda's shoulder. "And you, too, Amanda," she said. "You're very good at investigating too. I was just wondering if maybe you and David might like to do some investigating for a little while. You could interview the victims with David's tape recorder and take pictures with your camera and all kinds of things like that. Dad wouldn't care if you did it. He didn't say you couldn't be detectives."

Amanda laughed sarcastically. "Get outta here, kid," she said. "Count me out."

"David?" Janie said in a really pathetic tone of voice.

"Look, Janie, I don't—" David began when all of a sudden he happened to look at Garvey, and what he saw made him forget what he'd been about to say. Garvey seemed to be frozen with his spoon halfway to his mouth, and there was a startled look on his face.

"Hey," he said suddenly, "I just got an idea."

David chuckled. No wonder Garvey looked so surprised. Getting ideas wasn't something that happened to him on a regular basis. David glanced at Amanda and she glanced back, rolling her eyes and grinning.

"Hey," she said. "Guess what, everybody. Garvey has an idea."

"Yeah," Pete said enthusiastically. "I got me a great idea."

Carefully not looking at Amanda, David managed to stop smiling. "Okay, Garvey," he said. "Shoot. Let us in on the secret."

"We can investigate the missing mutts for our news story for Edmonds. And—and we can talk to old lady Ferris and them other people whose dogs got nabbed and—and—stuff like that."

It was David's turn to be surprised. It wasn't a bad idea after all. It was exactly what Mr. Edmonds wanted, an important local issue with lots of human interest. Everybody liked stories about dogs.

"Hey, Garvey," he said, "I think you've got something there."

"Yeah," Amanda said. "That sounds like a blast. I did some interviews when I was in Edmonds's class and it was fun. I'm great at that interviewing stuff." Holding up her spoon like a microphone, she said, "Good morning, ladies and gentlemen. This is Amanda Randall with station S-N-O-O-P. Today I'm talking with the victims of the mad dog-snatcher of Steven's Corners."

Garvey was staring at Amanda as if she really were some famous announcer, and even Janie seemed impressed. "Yes. Yes," she said nodding her head. "Just like that. That's great, Amanda. I think it's a wonderful idea. Pete and David can write their story for Mr. Edmonds and you can help with the snooping. And when we find the dogs we can take their pictures, and—"

"Wait a minute," David said. "What do you mean with that 'we' stuff? Remember what Dad said. *You* have to keep out of this."

Janie was still balancing on her tiptoes, and the look on her face gave David a sinking feeling.

"Promise?" he said. "If Pete and I get involved do you promise to keep out of this?"

"I *do*! I *do*!" Janie said.

Afterward David remembered that Janie was still standing on her tiptoes when she promised, but he couldn't remember where her hands were. He wished he'd remembered to notice if they were behind her back, where maybe she was hiding something—like crossed fingers.

Chapter 6

On the last Saturday of Christmas vacation David was feeling bored with just hanging out, so he decided to ride into Steven's Corners on his bicycle. It was early afternoon when he went looking for someone to ask and found Dad in Molly's studio, kibitzing while she painted.

"You too? What's this sudden yearning for urban life?" Dad asked before he got around to saying okay. It seemed that Amanda had already gone in on the bus to go shopping at the mall, and Janie and the twins had been after Dad to drive them in.

"Beats me," David said. "The lure of life in the fast lane, I guess." Which was kind of a joke, considering what a one-horse town Steven's Corners was.

Dad laughed and said to give his regards to Broadway and a few minutes later David was pedaling peacefully down the driveway when a voice screamed "STOP!"

and Janie dashed out from behind the rosebushes and threw herself right in front of him. Slamming on the brakes, he skidded sideways and wound up sitting in the driveway with his bicycle on top of him.

"Holy cow, Janie!" he yelled. "What did you do that for? I almost ran over you."

"Oh, thank you, David." Janie was doing her phony sweet and innocent bit. "Thank you for not running over me. I just had to talk to you before you went away. Here, let me help." And she grabbed the handlebars and pulled the bike up onto its wheels.

David's knee was hurting like crazy. He pulled up his pants leg to see if he was going to bleed to death or anything. It turned out that it was mostly just bruised, but he was still pretty angry. "You wanted to *talk*!" he more or less bellowed. "That's no reason to do a dumb thing like that."

Janie did a shocked and terrified number, making her eyes wide and letting her mouth drop open. He knew it was just an act, that Janie wasn't really afraid of him—as far as he knew, Janie Stanley wasn't really afraid of anything much—but her big act did tend to make him feel a little guilty.

"Well, tell me," he said, still examining his knee. "Why was talking to me so important you'd risk your stupid neck, not to mention mine?"

He'd hardly finished asking before he knew the answer, and wished he hadn't asked. The answer was going to have something to do with the missing-dogs thing. Since New Year's morning Janie had been pestering him constantly to get busy on the investigation, even though he'd tried to explain to her why he wanted to wait until after school started.

His main reason was that it was still vacation, and he didn't want to use up good vacation time on a school project, especially one that included a joint writing assignment with Pete Garvey. Not that old Pete didn't have his strong points, but David was pretty certain that literary composition wasn't one of them. But none of David's reasons and explanations made any impression on Janie. She'd gone right on following him around, begging him to get started, until he'd gotten mad and yelled at her. After that she just followed him around looking sad and wistful.

"I'm awfully sorry about your knee," she was saying now. "I just wanted to make a little suggestion before you left. I wanted to suggest that you stop by Pete's house on your way to—to wherever you're going, and make some plans about your interviews. You know; for your newspaper article."

"I was going downtown, and Pete's house is *not* on the way." David was still sitting on the ground inspecting his knee.

"Oh, yes it is. It *is*!" Janie said. "If you take the short-cut through the Wileys' orchard. Here, let me show you."

She let go of the bike and squatted down in the dirt.

"Look out!" David yelled. *"Ow!* Janie, you idiot!"

"See, you just turn off here at Wiley Lane and— what's the matter, David?"

"Oh, nothing at all," David said crawling out from under his bike. "You just dropped the bike on top of me, that's all."

"Oh, I'm sorry, David. I didn't mean to. But just look at this map I'm drawing. I'm showing you the shortcut to the Garveys' house."

"Forget it." David climbed back on his bike. "I've known that way for years. I'd call it more of a long-cut."

"But David"—Janie's voice had gone quivery and pitiful—"it's awfully important that we—"

"Okay, okay!" David interrupted. "I'll go that way. And I'll stop by and see if Garvey's at home. All right? Just get off my back. Okay?"

"Oh yes! Oh, that's wonderful. Here wait a minute." Janie reached into the pocket of her jacket. "Here's your tape recorder. If you get started on your investigation today you'll probably need it."

"*Janie!*" David said, grabbing the recorder out of her hand. "What are you doing with—" He stopped, turning his question into a sigh. He knew the answer. Janie had his tape recorder because she thought she was going to con him into starting work on the dog story today. "Forget it," he said, not looking at Janie in order not to notice her quivering lip and watery eyes. "I'm not going to waste a perfectly good Saturday. So just forget it. Okay?"

He shoved the tape recorder into his pocket and pedaled off, musing angrily about what a wimp Janie must think he was and how wrong she was and how he wasn't going to let himself be pushed around by any pint-size eight-year-old kid sister. He was still thinking about how wrong Janie was when he turned off Westerly Road onto Wiley Lane. When he realized what he was doing he explained it by telling himself wasn't really going to start work on the project. He was just going to stop by the Garveys' chicken ranch for a minute to maybe make a few plans with Pete about a date to begin the first interview—sometime next week. And besides, Pete probably wouldn't even be at home.

It turned out, he wasn't at home, at least not at first. When David finally pedaled past the long row of enormous chicken sheds and turned in at the drive that led to the Garveys' house, he found a woman chopping weeds in the front yard. It had to be Mrs. Garvey. He'd never been to the Garvey house before and he'd never met Pete's parents, but the woman in the front yard was as big as Pete and almost as homely. David was just standing there feeling a little surprised—somehow Garvey wasn't the kind of person you thought of as having had an actual mother—when the woman looked up and saw him.

"Who are you?" she said in a suspicious tone of voice. "Junior's not at home."

"Uh, hello, Mrs. Garvey," David said. "I'm—I'm David. David Stanley." The woman was coming toward him with a fierce frown on her face and her hoe up over her shoulder, as if she were getting ready to swing it at something taller than a weed. He took a quick step backward and swung his leg over his bicycle.

But then, suddenly, everything changed. "Stanley?" Mrs. Garvey said, as if something had finally registered. "David Stanley? Oh yes. Well why didn't you say so? Heard a lot about you around here, boy. Get down off that bike and come right in and have a piece of cake."

He really didn't want to, but Mrs. Garvey looked like the kind of person who might not take no for an answer. So a few minutes later he found himself sitting in the

Garveys' kitchen in front of an enormous piece of chocolate cake and listening to Mrs. Garvey tell him about
Peter Cornelius Garvey II. And having a hard time
keeping a straight face every time she referred to
mean, tough, bad old Garvey as Junior.

Mrs. Garvey really seemed to be happy about the
newswriting assignment and how David and Junior
were going to work on it together. She kept telling
David how pleased she was, and how she wished that all
of Junior's friends were interested in things like school
projects.

It seemed that Mrs. Garvey was worried about some
of Junior's friends. "That Maillard bunch was bad
enough," she said. "You know that bunch of good-for-
nothings?"

"Ace?" David asked. "I know Ace Maillard." You
couldn't go to Wilson Junior High and not know who
Ace was. Ace had quite a reputation at Wilson, and he
used to be considered Pete's best friend, before David
got drafted into the role.

"And his brother?" Mrs. Garvey went on. "Ace is bad
enough, but his brother is a real hood already. Mack,
they call him, I think."

David nodded. He'd heard about Mack Maillard, a
high-school dropout and car-crazy type who was always
roaring around town in souped-up cars or destroying
the hillsides around town on dirt bikes. "I've heard
about Mack," he said, grinning, "but the closest I've
come to meeting him was once when he ran me into a
ditch on my bicycle."

"Hmph! Just like him," Mrs. Garvey said. "And now
there's this new Potter bunch who look to be as bad as

the Maillards, if not worse. Roughnecks and hoods, all of them. Don't think about anything but drinking and carousing, and cars. They're all car crazy, the whole bunch of them."

Mrs. Garvey sat down at her kitchen table and brushed crumbs off the cracked and stained Formica with her big strong hands. Her face looked tired and sad.

"Junior is a good boy," she said. "Leastways, he used to be, before he started hanging around with them good-for-nothings. I just been so worried about him lately that—"

Before Mrs. Garvey could say any more, she was interrupted by what sounded like the whole Indianapolis 500 roaring down the driveway. Brakes screeched and a motor died, coughing and gasping. A car door slammed. Loud voices yelled and hooted as the engine sputtered back to life. In a moment the sputter built to a roar, tires squealed, and a cloud of dust drifted by the kitchen window. David and Mrs. Garvey were still staring at the drifting dust when the kitchen door banged open and Pete walked in.

"Hey, Stanley," he said, looking surprised. "What you doing here?"

"He's here about your school project," Mrs. Garvey said before David could answer. "So you just sit down here and have a little bite of cake and talk it over, and I'll get back to work." Smiling a wide toothy smile just like Pete's except without the chipped teeth, Mrs. Garvey put an even bigger piece of chocolate cake on the table and then disappeared out the back door.

For a minute, they ate in silence. David was telling

himself that he'd better resist the urge to call Garvey "Junior" if he knew what was good for him. He was still fighting the temptation, and maybe grinning a little, when all of a sudden Garvey said, "Okay, Stanley, get it over with. I'll give you one time. But after that, you call me Junior again and I'll launch you into orbit."

David's grin widened. Then he straightened out his face and said, "Okay, Junior. What about this newswriting assignment? You still interested in doing the missing-dogs thing?"

Garvey grinned back. "Yeah, Davey," he said. "What about it? Did you see the story in the *Valley Press* yesterday? Looks like someone's beat us to the draw. Maybe we better pick something else to write about."

David couldn't believe it. "Something else?" he said. "Why?" Not that he was looking forward to a joint project with Garvey. It was just that if they were going to have to work together on something, the dog story sounded more interesting than most. Not to mention the fact that it might get Janie off his back.

But when Garvey showed him the article in the *Valley Press* he saw that there was nothing to worry about. It was only a little squib saying that Mrs. Evangeline Ferris had reported the loss of her purebred poodle, and that it seemed to be part of a recent rash of dog thefts in the neighborhood.

"Oh, this little article won't make any difference," he told Garvey. "What we're going to do is some real investigative reporting, with interviews and photographs, and maybe if we're lucky an exposé of the culprits."

"A what?" Garvey said frowning.

"You know. We'll tell who's been doing the stealing."

"Oh yeah," Pete said, but then he frowned again. "But your kid sister won't like it much if it turns out to be them Chinese friends of hers after all."

"Vietnamese," David said, "And Janie says they're not doing it, and she probably knows. She's been at their house quite a bit, and she's . . . well, Janie is . . ."

"Yeah. I know," Pete said, grinning. "Janie is some kinda brain."

After that they talked about when they were going to begin. Although David pushed for Monday afternoon, Garvey seemed anxious to get started right away. And when he heard that David was on his way into town, he immediately insisted on getting out his bike and coming along and maybe getting started on the interviews.

"Come on," he said. "Let's get started grilling old lady Ferris."

"But don't you think Monday would be . . ." David began, but Garvey was already getting back into his jacket and heading for the door.

"But I didn't bring a camera," David protested. "I thought we wanted to take pictures."

"That's okay. I got one. We can use my camera today. Here's your jacket. Okay?"

Garvey held out David's jacket, and there was a look in his eyes that suggested that if David didn't put it on he might get stuffed into it.

David shrugged. "Well, if that's the way you feel about it," he said, and put on his jacket. Then he went on outside while Garvey went to get his camera.

Pete's mother was still in the front yard. David waved and called, "Good-bye, Mrs. Garvey; that sure was good cake," and she waved back and said for David to come again soon and he said he would. And when Pete came out she yelled for Junior to "come over here a minute before you go traipsing off again." David went on down the driveway.

He was still standing by the edge of the road waiting for Pete when a distant humming sound grew with unbelievable suddenness into a mind-boggling roar, and a car raced past him at what seemed to be about one hundred miles an hour. It had happened so fast that he didn't get a good look at the guys inside it, but he was pretty sure he knew who it must have been.

"Was that Mack Maillard?" he asked when Pete joined him at the edge of the road a minute later.

"Naw," Pete said. "Not driving, anyway. Mack has a street rod sort of like that, but that one belongs to Normy Potter. But Mack was with him, and so was Ace and Normy's brother. I was with them too until they dropped me off at the house. We been down to the drag strip. You know the Potters?"

David didn't, except for what Mrs. Garvey had said, so Pete told him about them as they pedaled down the road. It seemed the Potters had moved into the house at the old Springer dairy on the other side of town. There were two Potter brothers, and they were special friends of Mack Maillard's. LeRoy and Normy Potter, Garvey said, were real wheel freaks, and they had the fastest customized street rods and the best dirt bikes in the whole valley.

David didn't know much about rods, or dirt bikes either, but he was properly impressed. "I'm properly impressed," he told Garvey. "And if Normy had been about six inches to the right the impression might have been permanent." Garvey didn't seem to get the joke.

They were passing the Wiley orchard a few minutes later when Pete suddenly screeched to a stop. "Hey," he said, as if it had just occurred to him. "Maybe we ought to go by your place and see if Amanda wants to come along. You know, like she told Janie, she'd be good at the interviewing part of it."

"Amanda's not at home," David said, swallowing his grin. "She went into town to shop at the mall with a couple of her friends. She got some money for Christmas, and it's been burning a hole in her pocket." Pete looked so disappointed that he added, "Maybe we'll run into her in town. We could go past the mall on the way to the Ferris house."

"Yeah," Pete said. "Okay. We'll go past the mall." And he rattled off, grinning happily.

Even though David hated to interrupt Garvey's daydreams, he finally pedaled up alongside and brought up the subject of the interview. He was wondering, he said, what they might be able to accomplish on such short notice. He mentioned that they really should have prepared a list of questions to ask Mrs. Ferris. Otherwise they'd probably forget to ask about some of the most important details.

"Oh, that's okay," Pete said. "We probably won't get a chance to ask any questions anyway."

"What do you mean? Why won't we get to ask any questions? That's what we're going there for, isn't it?"

Garvey turned to look over his shoulder. "You ever met old lady Ferris?"

"No," David said.

"Thought not," Garvey said, and pedaled off, grinning his chipped-toothed grin.

Chapter 7

When David and Garvey got to town they turned onto
Main Street and cruised on down as far as the Wagon
Wheel Mall. At the mall parking lot Garvey stopped
and got off his bike. David circled around him, grinning.

"What are we stopping for?" he asked, as if he didn't
know. "I thought you said you just wanted to ride past."

"Yeah," Garvey said. "But I remembered something.
I just remembered . . ." He paused, looking pained.
Garvey always looked pained when he was trying to
come up with an idea. After a minute or two his fore-
head unwrinkled. "Yeah. I just remembered something
I want to buy. In the mall."

David circled at a safer distance. "That right? What
do you want to buy, Junior?"

Garvey's head lowered like a bull about to charge,
and David quickly enlarged his circle. He might have

been in trouble but just then, in the nick of time, Amanda appeared at the mall entrance. She was with Tammy and Eloise, her two best friends. They were all carrying Banana Republic shopping bags, and Amanda was wearing a new tent-shaped canvas jumper with khaki-colored long johns hanging out from under it.

Actually, David thought she looked pretty weird, but old Pete was staring at her as if she were some kind of famous celebrity. Maybe the whole outfit was kind of stylish, if you were into the trekking-through-darkest-Hollywood look. However, Amanda in long johns wasn't exactly what David thought of as dream girl material. And the expression on her face didn't improve the overall effect.

"Oh great! My prayers are answered," she said in her most sarcastic tone of voice. "My two favorite people in all the world." Then she turned her back and went on talking to her friends.

She probably would have gone right on ignoring them, except that as soon as Tammy, the plump friend with frizzy hair, noticed them she came right over. Tammy always acted as if she had a crush on Garvey, flirting with him and calling him "the Junior High Hunk" and things like that. Amanda went on talking to Eloise, but she kept checking to see what Tammy was doing, and after a few minutes she started edging in their direction.

David wasn't surprised, because the only thing Amanda seemed to hate more than having Pete Garvey hanging around was to have Tammy hanging around Pete Garvey. When she got to where David and Pete were sitting on their bicycles she said, "Well, what's on you dudes' so-called minds?"

Garvey had gone silent and glassy-eyed, so David explained that they were on their way to interview Mrs. Ferris, and to his surprise Amanda right away said that she was coming too. She gave Eloise, the thin one with the purple eyelids, all her shopping bags and told her to take them home with her. "I'll be over to pick them up later," she said. "When I'm through helping these two nerds with their newspaper reporting assignment for Mr. Edmonds. Remember that assignment last year?"

Tammy and Eloise both groaned and sighed and said they sure did, and, *man* were they ever glad that they were finished with Wilson Junior High and Mr. Edmonds, and *man* was it ever a lot better being in high school. And then they went off carrying Amanda's stuff, and Amanda got on the back of Garvey's bicycle.

Of course, Amanda had to put her arms around Garvey in order to hang on, and David had to fight a grin every time he got a look at Garvey's face. There was this kind of stunned expression, like he'd just made a ninety-yard touchdown run or maybe won the lottery jackpot. But poor old Garvey's seventh heaven didn't last very long, because they didn't have far to go.

It was only a few minutes by bicycle to where Mrs. Ferris lived on Baker Street, in the old part of Steven's Corners. Her house was a big old brown shingle set far back from the street, with a large garden in front. The three of them got off the two bikes and stood there for a while outside the front gate. The garden was a jungle of untrimmed bushes and low-hanging trees, and the iron fence around it was tall and strong and solid-looking.

"I don't see how that poodle could have just run away," Amanda said. "At least, not unless someone left the gate open. That's a good strong fence."

"Yeah. An important clue," David said. He took out his recorder and taped, "Strong fence. Missing poodle probably could not have gotten out by itself."

They stood there a while longer looking through the fence into the overgrown garden. David was wishing again that he'd known ahead of time that they were going to do the interviewing today, which made him remember what Pete had said about not needing to have a list of questions.

"Why did you say we wouldn't need a list of questions?" he asked.

Pete shrugged. "I dunno. Old lady Ferris is kind of wacky. Talks a lot. Yells, too. Bet we don't get a chance to ask much."

"Great," David said. Telling himself that they might as well get it over with, he reached inside for the latch and pushed the gate open. It moved stiffly, making a high-pitched grating screech that went down his backbone like the sound of fingernails on a blackboard. When he motioned for Pete and Amanda to go on in they just stood there looking at him, so he stepped around the partly open gate and led the way.

A winding brick path led to the front porch, but trees and bushes had crowded it into a dim, narrow tunnel. Several times they had to duck low-hanging branches or push aside dangling vines. Amanda was giggling in a nervous sort of way. They were almost at the front porch steps when she said, "Hey, this is weird. Gives me the creeps. Let's get out of here, okay?"

"Yeah!" Garvey's whisper was loud and raspy. "I'll go with you. Want to, Amanda?"

"Well, wait a minute," David said. "We're already this far. I think we should—" Before he could finish the sentence he was interrupted by a crackling noise that seemed to come from directly behind him. He whirled around to face a terrifying sight.

Not three feet away a wild-looking old woman was standing in the middle of the path swinging a huge curved sword around her head. Her long gray hair was flying in all directions, her eyes were wide and staring, and from her open mouth came a steady stream of screeching noises. It took David several seconds to recognize the sounds as words, and by then he and Pete and Amanda were all cringing back as far as they could get into the vines and bushes.

"Caught you! Caught you this time! Thought you could come back again and get my other babies, didn't you? But I caught you in the act, you kidnappers, you heartless thieving kidnappers, you. . . ."

"Ma'am—ma'am, could I just explain," David had started saying, but it wasn't doing any good because the woman was screaming too steadily to hear anything. There was no telling what would have happened if she'd hadn't screeched herself into a kind of choking fit. It was while she was struggling to get her breath back that David climbed out of the bush he'd backed into and went on trying to get her to listen to his explanation.

"We're not the dog thieves," he kept saying. "We just came to interview you for the school paper. Honestly. We're not the ones who took your dog."

The old woman, who was, of course, Mrs. Ferris, had stopped swinging her machete and was clutching her chest instead. She was still choking a little, so David started patting her on the back, while he went on repeating who they were and what they were doing in her yard. At last the choking fit wound up in a series of little gasps, and the old woman stared at David for a minute, a long, searching look, that felt like it was X-raying his brain. Then she handed him the machete.

"Well, why didn't you say so," she said sharply. "Here, hold this while I make myself presentable. Blackberry bush snagged my hairnet while I was creeping up on you." She was smoothing down her hair when she noticed that Pete and Amanda were still plastered into the underbrush. "Well now, don't the two of you look silly," she said. "Come on out of there and introduce yourselves."

While Pete and Amanda were getting themselves untangled from the bushes, Mrs. Ferris looked at an old-fashioned watch that hung around her neck on a chain. "Well, look at that," she said. "It's teatime. We might as well go right on in and have a cup of tea while we talk about this newspaper story."

The old woman led the way on up the path and across the wide front porch, followed by a pale-looking Amanda and a very quiet Pete. David brought up the rear, feeling a little shaky himself now that the crisis was over.

A few minutes later the three of them were waiting in the living room of the Ferris house while Mrs. Ferris prepared the tea. Still clutching the machete, David was sitting beside Pete on a high-backed sofa in a room that looked like something out of an oriental painting. Across from them in an elaborately carved chair Amanda sat stiffly, still pale and silent.

Finally Garvey cleared his throat and said in a hoarse whisper. "For a minute there I thought we'd had it."

"Yeah," David said. "Some welcome. And look at this place. Did you know about this house? Looks like some kind of museum. You ever been in here before?"

Garvey looked around. "Naw. I heard she had a weird house but I never been in it before. Look at that!"

The dimly lit room, darkened by heavy red brocade drapes, was crowded with all kinds of oriental-style furniture and ornaments. Painted and embroidered hangings and tapestries covered the walls, Chinese lanterns hung from the ceiling, and all around the room fat gilded Buddhas and other oriental statues sat on pedestals or in whatnot cupboards. Hanging above the fireplace was a display of ornately decorated weapons: swords in gold-embroidered scabbards, spears hung with silken tassels, and two or three vicious-looking daggers. Noticing a couple of empty hooks below a machete-shaped dark spot on the wall, David got up and put the weapon back where it belonged.

"A bit to the left," Mrs. Ferris said, coming into the room carrying a tray. She put the tray on a small inlaid game table and came over to the fireplace, watching with approval while he rearranged the machete. Then they all sat down and had tea and tiny crisp wafers that tasted something like fortune cookies.

After a while David began to enjoy himself. Watching both Garvey and Amanda drinking tea, which Amanda always said she hated and which Garvey probably did, too, and munching daintily on the tiny cookies, David kept having to squelch a grin.

As soon as the tea was finished David got out his tape recorder and asked Mrs. Ferris if it would be all right if he taped the conversation, and that was almost the last question he got to ask. Garvey had been right about not needing any. Without any prompting at all Mrs. Ferris gave them all kinds of information about the disappearance of Phoebe, and about a lot of other stuff, too, including all the strange things in her living room.

It seemed that Mrs. Ferris's late husband had been an importer who did most of his business in the Far East, which explained all the oriental stuff. She went on for quite a while about the furniture and decorations, telling them which country everything was from and how long she'd had it. She'd finally stopped talking about the furniture and was just beginning to get into Phoebe's disappearance when David began to be aware of a strange snuffling, whimpering noise. He waited until Mrs. Ferris slowed up a bit to catch her breath and managed to say, "What's that?"

"What's what?" Mrs. Ferris said.

"That funny noise."

She listened for a minute and then jumped to her feet. "Why, that's the rest of my babies," she said. "They want to come in and meet the company. Why, of course they do. Come right on in, darlings, and meet these nice young people from the school paper."

The moment Mrs. Ferris got the door open the whole room seemed to be full of poodles. There was a big one named Lucinda and another called Maximus. One of them was white and the other was black, but David didn't get it straight right away which was which. The rest of them were half grown puppies, and some of them were black and some were white and they were all super friendly. Before long David had a puppy in his lap and so did Pete, and Amanda had two. It took a while to get back to the subject of the missing dog and how and when she disappeared, but when they finally did, David was able to tape a lot of important information.

According to Mrs. Ferris, Phoebe was a very valuable —not to mention intelligent, adorable, devoted, and obedient—poodle. An apricot poodle, she said, very special and expensive. And she had disappeared right out of the fenced yard at about eight P.M., on Friday, the nineteenth of December.

"I'd just let them all out for their last little run before bedtime," Mrs. Ferris said, "and just as I was opening the door to call them back in, I heard a sharp little yelp, which I recognized immediately as Phoebe's—and Phoebe in trouble, I might add. I know all my babies' voices and what they're trying to tell me, and Phoebe was saying she was frightened. So I ran down the steps calling to her, and I heard her yelp again in a muffled way, as if someone might have been holding her muzzle, and then there was the sound of the gate slamming and people running, at least two people and maybe more. But by the time I got to the gate there was no one in sight. No one. And my poor little Phoebe was gone."

Mrs. Ferris's voice had started to tremble. She got out a handkerchief and began to mop her eyes, and Lucinda and Maximus came over to her and put their forepaws in her lap and licked her face, as if they were trying to comfort her. David put down his puppy and went over to her too. He was just standing there, trying to think what to say, when Garvey said, "Don't you worry no more about it, Mrs. Ferris. We're going to find out who done it."

Garvey's voice sounded strange, and when Amanda started talking, hers did too. "We sure are, Mrs. Ferris," she said. "You can count on us."

David couldn't think of anything to add, so he just stood there, wondering if he ought to pat her on the shoulder or something. But he didn't, and after a while she calmed down and Pete got out his camera and took some pictures, and then they all said good-bye.

It was while they were on their way out to the gate that David noticed that Amanda and Garvey were both acting shifty-eyed and embarrassed.

Nobody said anything until just before they got to the gate, and then Amanda shrugged and laughed in an offhand kind of way and said, "What a scene! We're lucky we didn't get our heads chopped off," and Garvey snorted and said, "Yeah, I thought we were goners for sure." They went on like that for a while, about how crazy Mrs. Ferris was and how they didn't know if they'd come closer to being macheteed or talked to death.

"Well, I thought she was kind of neat," David said angrily, and then, of course, they both jumped on him.

"Davey thinks Mrs. Ferris is kind of neat," Amanda said in a prissy tone of voice. "Davey thinks bunnies and teddy bears and crazy old ladies are kind of neat."

Garvey laughed and said, "Yeah, Davey's a pushover

for stuff like that," which was obviously just kissing up to Amanda, besides being a stupid remark. Clenching his teeth, David pushed past the two of them and went on out the gate, slamming it behind him. He got on his bike and was starting off when Garvey grabbed the back of his bicycle and pulled him to a stop.

"Whoa there, Stanley," he said.

"Where do you think you're going?" Amanda said.

"Home, I guess," David said, without turning around.

"You giving up so soon?"

"What do you mean 'so soon'?" David asked.

"Before we finish our investigation. We got time to do at least one more interview today. We could do that Boggs family next, that live out in Steven's Heights."

"Yeah," Amanda said. "Why don't we go to the Boggses'?"

David turned around and glared at both of them. "Forget it," he said. "I'm not going anywhere with the two of you."

"Oh come on, David," Amanda said. "We were just kidding. And besides, we really need you. You're the one with the tape recorder and all the good ideas about questions and stuff."

"Yeah," Garvey said, grinning. "You're the brains of this mob. You know, like Humphrey Bogart in that gangster movie."

"Besides," Amanda said. "If you quit on us now I might even punch you one."

Garvey's grin turned into a leer. "Yeah, me too. I'll mash you flatter than a—"

"Shut up, Garvey," Amanda said. "He's my brother.

If he needs punching, I'll do it. You keep your hands to yourself."

Garvey's leer deflated like a leaky balloon. Hiding a smile, David climbed on his bicycle and started off toward Steven's Heights.

Chapter 8

The Boggses lived in Steven's Heights, the new housing development in the foothills just outside of town. David didn't know the exact address but he'd expected that Garvey would. They were halfway up the first steep hill between rows of imitation Victorians and Mexican haciendas when he found out otherwise.

"Who me?" Garvey said. "I don't know nothing about these new houses. All look alike to me."

"Great!" Amanda said. "What'll we do now?"

"I don't know," David said. "Unless we . . ." He looked around. "Unless we ask somebody?"

"Like who?"

"Well, how about those two little kids on the tricycles."

"Those little dudes?" Amanda said. "I doubt if they know where they live themselves."

The two little dudes were pedaling up and down a

driveway making loud engine noises and yelling "Honk-honk" at each other. It was hard to get their attention, but when they finally tuned in to what David was asking they were eager to help. But Amanda was right. They weren't exactly the Steven's Heights information bureau.

"Boggs?" the littler one said, looking blank. "Who's Boggs?"

"Boggs is Billy's name, you dumbhead," his friend said. "Don't you know nothing? Billy Boggs." He turned back to David. "At Billy's house," he said with a smug smile. "The Boggses live at Billy's house."

"We know that, wimp," Amanda said. "But where is it? Which one of these houses belongs to your pal Billy?"

The little kid thought for a while before he answered. "Billy's not my pal," he said. "Billy kicks me."

David laughed. "That's the one, all right. Janie's been talking about him all year. You know; the kid in her class that takes karate and goes around kicking people for practice."

"Not to mention spreading lies about people," Amanda said. "This kid sounds like a real winner."

"Okay, you guys," David said. "Could either of you show us the house where Billy Boggs lives?"

"Oh!" the little boys said in unison, in a why-didn't-you-say-so tone of voice, and then they both pointed up the hill.

"Right there. The yellow one," the bigger kid said.

"With all the kids," his friend added.

Sure enough, the fifth or sixth house up the road was yellow and the front yard was full of kids. At least seven or eight of them seemed to be crawling around on the lawn. David thanked the two little tricycle riders and got back on his bike. The road was so steep that it was slow going, and it wasn't until he had almost reached the yellow house that he really checked out the people in the Boggs front yard.

By his size and the karate-type scowl on his face, the one who was sitting on the front steps was probably the famous Billy himself. The others, who were crawling around on the ground as if they were looking for something, were all smaller. And on closer observation some of them were . . .

"Look," David said to Pete and Amanda. "It's Janie and the twins. And the Vietnamese kids too."

"Yeah," Amanda said. "What's Janie doing here? I thought she hated the Karate Kid."

"She does," David said. "At least, she always says she does."

They were almost there when Janie noticed them and jumped to her feet. "Hi David," she said, running down the steeply sloping lawn. "Hi Amanda. Hi Pete. Did you come to do the investigation after all? You said you weren't going to."

"I changed my mind," David said. "But what I want to know is, what are you doing here? You promised, no more private eye stuff. Remember?"

"Oh, we're not doing private eye stuff," Janie said quickly. "We're just playing. We came to play with Billy."

Lowering his voice David said, "I thought you hated Billy Boggs. I thought you said he was the meanest kid in your class."

"No, I didn't," Janie said. "I just said Billy likes to practice his karate on people. And he doesn't practice on me anymore."

"Oh yeah?" Amanda said. "Why not?"

"Because I told him I have a secret file on him, and that if he kicks me one more time I'll turn it over to the CIA. He hasn't kicked me even once since I told him about what the CIA would do to him."

It was a good story, David thought, but he still had some questions that needed answers. He started to ask why they'd all been crawling around on the lawn, when Esther came running and sliding down the steep slope.

"Hi," she said. "Did you see what we're doing? We were—"

"We were playing, Tesser," Janie said loudly. "We're playing a game." She gave Esther a hard, squinty-eyed look.

"Oh, yes," Esther said. "We're playing . . ." She stopped, rolling her eyes desperately toward Janie. "We were playing . . ."

"Find the thimble," Janie said, and Esther nodded, looking relieved. "Yes. We were playing find the thimble. That's why we were looking through the grass. We were looking for a thimble."

"The game," Amanda said, "is hide the thimble. I've never heard of find the thimble."

"Well," Janie said, "hide the thimble is the first part of the game. But after you hide it you have to find it. That's what we were doing. The second part."

"I give up," Amanda said, throwing up her hands and walking away.

David didn't blame her; arguing with Janie didn't

usually get you anywhere. But this time David didn't intend to let her off so easy. It was pretty obvious that she was breaking her promise about no more detective stuff, and he was going to get her to admit it.

Just then a woman came out onto the porch, a skinny woman wearing tight orange slacks and lots of makeup. She put up her hand to shade her eyes and stood there staring down across the lawn with a worried expression on her face. David thought he knew why. It was probably because of Garvey. To have something that looked like Pete Garvey suddenly appear on your front lawn was enough to worry anybody. David thought he'd better explain.

"Mrs. Boggs," he called. "Mrs. Boggs, could I talk to you a minute?"

He put down his bicycle and climbed up the steep lawn onto the front porch. As soon as he got there he started explaining about the story for the school paper and how their assignment was to investigate and write about the stolen dogs.

"I understand your dog was stolen just last week, is that right?" David asked.

"That's right. You say the story's going to be in the paper?"

"Well, just the school paper at first. But Mr. Edmonds says the *Valley Press* is going to use some of the best stories."

"There going to be pictures too?" Mrs. Boggs asked. "I take a real good picture." When David said yes she got even more interested. "Come right on in, the three of you. I'm sure Bud will want to talk to you too." She motioned for Pete and Amanda to follow and headed for the front door.

Before he went into the house, David checked out the little kids again. They'd stopped crawling around and were sitting in a circle on the lawn. Besides Janie and the twins and Thuy and Huy there were two others he didn't recognize; they looked like smaller versions of Billy and were probably his brothers. Janie was talking like crazy and waving her arms around and the other kids seemed to be absolutely hypnotized. Particularly the two little Boggses.

David grinned. Obviously those two hadn't met Janie before and didn't know what to make of her. Just as David was turning away Blair suddenly whirled around and smiled at him, as if something had told him David was watching. Blair did that kind of thing a lot.

The Boggs living room was full of oversize purple and black furniture and huge paintings of pinkish sunsets over the ocean. When Mrs. Boggs led David and Amanda and Pete into the room her husband—Bud, she'd called him—was watching wrestling on TV. He didn't seem too enthusiastic about being interrupted, but he finally shut off the TV when she started explaining about the news story—at least, he shut the sound off and only went on watching the picture a little bit, out of the corner of his eye. But as soon as the tape recorder was turned on he became almost as talkative as his wife.

Both the Boggses liked talking into the tape recorder. But at first they only wanted to talk about other things, not about their missing dog. Mrs. Boggs wanted to talk about how she studied to be a model once and was almost on the cover of a magazine. And Mr. Boggs wanted to talk about his company, the Boggs and Turner Development Company, and how it was going to build a big new shopping center in Steven's Corners as soon as they decided on the best location.

After David finally got the conversation around to the missing dog, the only problem was that now and then while other people were talking, Mr. Boggs would suddenly yell at one of the wrestlers. The first few times he yelled "KILL HIM!" or "BREAK HIS ARM!" David jumped about a foot, but after a while he got more or less used to it.

There were, it seemed, one or two similarities between the disappearance of Phoebe and that of Rambo, the Boggses' Doberman. Like Phoebe, Rambo had apparently been stolen on a Friday evening. But Rambo had been out all evening, tied to his doghouse in the back yard. He hadn't been missed until the next morning.

"And by then it was too late. There was nothing there except a little piece of the rope. The robbers cut it off right near the doghouse," Mrs. Boggs said.

"Are you sure he couldn't have chewed it off?" David asked.

"It was cut," Mr. Boggs said, "by something real sharp."

Amanda asked if Rambo would have gone off with a stranger without a struggle. "I've always heard that Dobermans were pretty fierce," she said. "Wouldn't he have put up a fight?"

"Haw!" Mr. Boggs said. "You'd think so, wouldn't you. But not Rambo. A real cream puff. To tell you the truth,

I'd have ditched him myself a long time ago if I hadn't paid so much for him."

"And if the kids weren't so crazy about him," Mrs. Boggs said.

Mr. Boggs shrugged. "Yeah, that too," he said.

It was about then that Billy, the karate expert, came in from the front porch, and from then on all the questions had to be answered by all three Boggses. With every answer in triplicate, the interview took quite a bit of time.

David and Amanda asked a few more questions, and even Garvey came up with a good one about sounds they might have heard on Friday night.

"You hear any running?" he asked. "Mrs. Ferris said she heard, like, a bunch of people running away."

"Nope. Didn't hear a thing except a little barking," Mr. Boggs said. "Sometimes Rambo barks for a long time, but that night he barked hard for a minute or two early in the evening, and then nothing. It got quiet, and we kinda forgot about it till the next morning."

"That's right," Mrs. Boggs said. "He barked real hard—"

"KILL HIM!" Mr. Boggs yelled suddenly. David almost dropped the tape recorder, but Mrs. Boggs didn't miss a beat.

"He barked real hard," she went right on. "We didn't think anything of it till the next day."

"Yeah," Billy said. "He barked real loud. Like this; listen. Rambo barked like this." And Billy started demonstrating how Rambo had barked. He insisted on barking into the tape recorder, and after he'd barked for a while he wanted to hear it played back. And then he wanted to do it again, and again, to get it just right. His parents started yelling at him to stop, but he just yelled back and went on barking. So after a while David turned off the tape recorder and said he thought they'd better be going.

"Anyway," Billy said when David put the tape recorder away. "We know who stole Rambo. Don't we, Dad?"

Everything got very quiet. "What?" Amanda said. "Who stole him, then?"

Billy looked at his father. "Tell them, Dad," he said.

"Well," Mr. Boggs said. "We don't want to have it put in the paper that we're accusing anyone. Let's just say we have our suspicions. All right. Let's just leave it at that for now. All *right*, Billy!"

They wouldn't say any more, so Garvey took a few pictures, with Mrs. Boggs posing herself carefully in all of them, and then Mr. and Mrs. Boggs walked them out to the front porch. They were saying good-bye when Mr. Boggs pointed and said, "What are those kids doing here? Billy, why didn't you tell me those kids were on our place?" He jumped off the porch and started down across the lawn, with Billy running after him.

From the porch David couldn't quite hear what Mr. Boggs said to the kids, but whatever it was it couldn't have been good. Janie and the twins and Thuy and Huy jumped up and backed off across the lawn looking surprised and frightened, and Mr. Boggs grabbed the two little Boggs kids and pulled them to their feet. When Janie and her gang got to the sidewalk Billy suddenly ran after them, jumping around and doing karate kicks in the air. But he really didn't connect with anybody, and when his father yelled at him he stopped and came back.

"Mrs. Boggs," Amanda said, "would you mind telling us what's going on?"

"It's not that we're prejudiced or anything," Mrs. Boggs said. "It's just that there's this rumor about that Vietnamese family, that they're the ones who've been stealing all the dogs. We don't want any of those Vietnamese hanging around. They're probably just casing the neighborhood for some more dogs to steal."

"Look, Mrs. Boggs," David said. "I think you're wrong about the Trans. Janie, my sister—the blond one down there—plays with the Tran kids a lot. And she's sure that they wouldn't think of stealing."

Mrs. Boggs stared at David and then at Janie, who was still standing on the sidewalk with the rest of the little kids. "That little tiny thing?" she said in a scornful tone of voice. "How old is she anyway? About five? What would she know about it?"

"She's eight, actually," David said. "And she knows a lot about . . ." It wouldn't be easy trying to explain Janie to a person like Mrs. Boggs. But he wanted to say something more, because he suddenly realized that while Mrs. Boggs might not believe Janie about the Trans, he certainly did.

He was still trying to think of something convincing to say when Amanda grabbed his arm. "Come on, David. Let's get out of here." She jumped off the porch and ran down across the lawn to the bicycles.

David and Garvey followed her, and a minute later they were coasting down the hill. Behind them they could hear the two little Boggs kids howling as their father dragged them up the lawn.

"Janie!" they were yelling. "We want to play with Janie."

Amanda laughed. "Listen to those kids. They must have been having a blast. I wonder what Janie was telling them."

David was wondering the same thing. And, speaking of Janie, where was she? And the rest of the kids? David slowed down and looked around. There was no one on the street or sidewalks that led down to the entrance of Steven's Heights. And there certainly hadn't been time for them to get farther than that.

"They're gone," he called to Amanda as she and Pete pulled ahead.

Pete circled and came back. "What's the matter, Stanley?" he asked.

"The little kids. Where'd they go?"

Amanda laughed. "Disappeared into thin air," she said. "Come on, David, let's go. They'll turn up."

"Yeah," David said, "I suppose they will. They always have." He pushed off and coasted on down the hill.

Chapter 9

Janie and the twins turned up all right. Less than an hour after David gave up looking for them in Steven's Heights they turned up on the city bus that went out Westerly Road.

David and Amanda were almost home at the time. Garvey had turned off at Wiley Lane and Amanda had gotten on behind David, and he was struggling up the last slope before home when the bus chugged past.

"Hey, look!" Amanda yelled in his ear. "There they are. The kids."

David braked his bike. He needed a breather anyway. Getting up hills with Amanda on behind hadn't seemed to bother Garvey, but then he was in love, and maybe that made a difference. The old city bus wheezed past and on up the hill, sounding as out of breath as David was.

And there, with their faces practically plastered to

one of the windows, were Janie and Esther and Blair. Waving and grinning from the bus window, they seemed delighted to see Amanda and David, but later, at closer range, they weren't nearly as enthusiastic. As a matter of fact, David definitely got the impression they were trying to avoid him.

He ran into Esther first in the downstairs hall. She seemed to be headed for the kitchen, but the minute she saw him she turned around and ran back up the stairs. And when he called to her to come back she said she was on her way to the bathroom *"in a hurry!"* She didn't come out of the bathroom for a long time.

Blair didn't try to get away when David found him in their room, but he wasn't exactly informative, either.

"Doing?" he said when David tried to question him. "What were we doing at the Boggses?" He smiled his Christmas-card-angel smile. "I guess we were playing?"

"Okay, but what? What were you playing?"

Blair tipped his head to one side and thought for a long time before he said, "Maybe I forgot." Then he nodded and smiled again. "Yes, I remember now. I forgot."

David sighed. "Holy cow, Blair. What does that mean? You remember you forgot."

"Don't be mad," Blair said. "I didn't forget on purpose. Janie made me."

"I'll bet she did," David said and went looking for Janie.

Janie was in the kitchen helping Molly make dinner. "What can I do now?" she asked Molly as David walked into the kitchen. "What else can I do to help?"

"Well . . ." Molly looked pleased, and surprised. "Let me see. I guess you could set the table."

"In the kitchen? Are we going to eat at the kitchen table? Let's do eat in here tonight. It's so much more friendly than the dining room."

Molly looked more surprised, and David had to hide a grin. Although the family ate breakfast and lunch in the kitchen, they usually had dinner at the big table in the dining room. But if Janie went into the dining room to set the table, David would have her cornered, and she knew it.

Of course Molly got talked into a friendly dinner in the kitchen, and so David had to back off and wait. He didn't ask Janie any questions during the meal, but Dad asked one that cleared up a couple of things. Like how the kids got to Steven's Heights. Dad's question was, "Well, how were things at the park?"

"Park?" Janie said, freezing with her spoon halfway to her mouth. The twins had stopped eating too and were staring at Janie. "Did you say at the park, Daddy?"

Amanda grinned and rolled her eyes at David, but she didn't say anything. David didn't really think she would. Amanda wasn't always the greatest as a stepsister, but she generally wasn't a tattletale.

"Yes." Dad went on. "I seem to remember being talked into driving the three of you in to play in the park this afternoon. Was your friend there, and did you play on the new equipment?"

"Oh, yes. Yes, Thuy was there, and the new jungle gym is lots of fun. We like the new jungle gym, don't we, twins?"

"Is that right? Do you like to climb on the jungle gym,

Blair?" Both Dad and Molly were smiling encouragingly. They always liked it when Blair did any normal-kid-type stuff, because he was usually so quiet and spacy.

"The jungle gym . . ." Blair said, tipping his head the way he always did when he was thinking. "The jungle gym is—"

"Actually," Janie interrupted, "we didn't stay at the park very long. All the new stuff was so crowded that we decided to walk up to Steven's Heights to visit another friend, who's in my class. So we played at the friend's house for a while and then Thuy and Huy went home and we caught the bus just like you said . . ."

Dad was frowning and David was expecting him to say something about getting permission to do one thing and then doing something else, and he probably would have, too, except that Janie just kept on going.

". . . and Daddy, you know what Thuy is doing? Thuy is memorizing the Declaration of Independence. Her parents are learning it in their class to become citizens, so she decided to learn it too. And she's teaching me. I already know, 'When in the course of human events it becomes necessary . . .' "

Janie hadn't actually learned the whole Declaration, but she knew enough of it to get everybody's mind off why she hadn't stayed at the park. After she finally ran down, Dad didn't ask her any more questions. David could understand why. Dad was probably afraid they might get the whole Constitution next. But David himself was still planning to do some asking as soon he got Janie alone.

His next attempt was in the living room after dinner,

but Janie immediately started talking to Dad again. Dad was trying to read the paper.

"I notice you're reading about interest rates," Janie said, leaning over Dad's shoulder. "Could you explain to me about interest rates, Daddy? That's something I've been wanting to learn about for a long time."

At first Dad frowned, and David thought he was about to tell Janie to clear out. He went on frowning while she squeezed under his arm and into his lap.

"I see here that they're going up," she said pointing to a headline. "What makes them go up, Daddy?"

Dad's frown began to change from bothered to professorial. "Well, perhaps it could be explained like this," he began, and David gave up and went to his room. When Dad got that look on his face he was good for an hour's lecture, at least.

It wasn't until just before bedtime that David managed to corner Janie in the upstairs hall. "Okay, I got you," he said pinning her against the wall by both shoulders. "I want a few answers." Janie tried to wiggle loose, but when she realized it was impossible she switched to super cooperative.

"All right, David," she said in a gushy tone of voice, like a hostess on a game show. "Ask me. Ask me the questions. Ask me any question you want."

"Well, first of all, why were you and the twins and the Tran kids at Billy Boggs's house?"

"And what else?" Janie said. "What other questions do you want to ask?"

"What were you doing on the lawn? Why you were all crawling around like that?"

"All right. Is that all?"

"Well, isn't that enough? Oh yes, one more thing. Where did you go after you left the Boggses'? You were right there on the sidewalk and then you just disappeared. Where did you get to so quickly?"

Janie smiled delightedly. "Wasn't that good? That was blending in. We're very good at blending in."

"What do you mean, 'blending in'?" David asked.

"You know, like when you're tailing someone and you try to look like a normal everyday person going about your business—like a shopper or a dog walker or something. So you won't be noticed."

"Oh yeah," David said. "But there weren't any people around for you to blend in with."

"Yes there were. Not on the sidewalk, but in the driveway of the house next door to the Boggses. There were these three little kids and we blended in with them."

"I didn't see any kids in the driveway."

"Well, actually they were in a car. These three little kids were in the back seat of a car waiting for their mother to come out and take them somewhere. So I just opened the back door and we all climbed in and blended with them. And then as soon as the danger was past I opened the other back door and we all climbed out."

"Wow!" David said. "Five, six, seven, *eight* kids in one back seat?"

Janie nodded. "It was pretty crowded. But that's the best way to blend. It's easier to blend in a crowd. And the three little kids weren't very big. Especially the baby."

"The baby?" David asked apprehensively. "There was a baby in that mess?"

"Umm! But we didn't squash it—much. Tesser sat on it a little, but not seriously." Janie sighed and then smiled triumphantly. "It was one of our best blendings. It really worked, didn't it?"

"Yeah, it worked I guess. We sure couldn't find you, at least. But how about the other questions I asked you? You were playing detective again, weren't you? After you promised Dad you wouldn't."

"Well . . ." She sighed again and rolled her eyes. "Well—*David! You're hurting me!*" She clutched her shoulder. "I think you just broke my clavichord."

David laughed. "Clavicle. You mean your clavicle." He let go of Janie's shoulders and she slumped to the floor.

"Well, it's broken, anyway," she whimpered. "Oh, oh! It hurts, David. It really hurts."

Janie moaned louder and Nightmare rushed out of David and Blair's room. When he saw Janie all crumpled up and moaning on the floor he trotted over and sniffed at her. He looked worried. For a dog, Nightmare was really good at worried expressions. Janie went on whimpering.

David patted Nightmare. "It's all right, big guy," he said. "I think she'll live. Come on, Janie. Knock it off. I didn't hurt you."

"You did. Yes, you did. I can't get up. I can't even stand up."

David knew he hadn't been holding Janie hard enough to hurt her. But just the same it was embarrassing, because she was so little and delicate-looking and he was so much bigger. "I didn't really hurt her," he found himself explaining to Nightmare. "She's just putting on an act." He grabbed Janie around the middle, stood her on her feet, and propelled her toward her room, with Nightmare following close behind.

In the girls' room Esther was sitting on the floor next to her dollhouse. "What's the matter? What's the matter?" she said as Janie limped and moaned into the room.

"David hurt me. He broke my clavichord." Janie limped to her bed and collapsed onto it. "I'm in terrible pain. Terrible!"

Nightmare was leaning over the bed snuffling at Janie's neck, and the last "terrible" turned into a giggle. "Stop it, Nightmare. That tickles."

Esther jumped up and ran to the bed. "Where? Where is it broken, Janie?"

"Here. Right here." Janie clutched her shoulder.

"That's where it's broken?" Esther looked puzzled. "Then why were you limping?"

"Good question," David said.

He'd had all he could take. He started out of the room, but halfway down the hall he changed his mind. She'd done it again. She'd gotten rid of him before he'd gotten the answers to his questions. This time he wasn't going to let her get away with it. He turned around and marched back to the girls' room. Janie was sitting on the edge of the bed with her arms around Nightmare's neck. "Oops!" she said, and collapsed again, holding her shoulder and scrunching her face into a suffering expression.

"Never mind," David said. "Knock off the dramatics. It won't work anymore."

Janie sighed and let her face go back to normal. "All right, all right. I'll answer all your qestions. But first there's something else I want to tell you. It's about the Trans."

"What about the Trans?"

"It's really awful. It's so terrible, David. Poor Thuy is so worried. It's about her father and his job. Mr. Tran is going to lose his job, and Thuy doesn't know what they're going to do. They'll have to move, because they live in that house at the nursery that belongs to his boss, and if he can't find another job they may even starve to death. And Mrs. Tran is so sad she cries all the time, because she'd so worried about not having enough money to buy food for all their children."

"All their children? How many do they have?"

"Four of them. Thuy and Huy and the two little ones."

"There are two littler than Huy?"

"Umm!" Janie nodded. "And Mr. Tran is going to lose his job because Mr. Wright, who owns the nursery, thinks he's been stealing dogs."

"Why does he think that?" David asked.

"Because people are saying so, I guess. He told Mr. Tran he didn't believe the rumors, but he still says he's about decided to sell the nursery. And Mr. Tran thinks it's because Mr. Wright thinks business will get bad because of what people are saying about the stolen dogs."

"Holy cow," David said. He sat down on the side of Janie's bed. Esther climbed up beside him, and then

Nightmare decided to climb up, too, and they all had to scoot around to make room for him. He went tromping around, all one hundred and sixty-five pounds of him, nearly bouncing the rest of them off the bed. He'd finally gotten settled when Esther began to cry, and he got up and rearranged himself so he could nuzzle Esther instead of Janie. He was looking sad and kind of bewildered, and you could certainly see why. David was feeling pretty much the same way.

"Stop it, Esther," he said. "What are you crying about?"

"A-a-about the Trans," Esther said. "I don't want them to starve to death."

"Esther," David said, "did you hear Thuy say that her father was going to lose his job? Did she really say that?"

Esther nodded, sobbing loudly. "Yes. Thuy said it."

David sighed. You couldn't always believe Janie's tears, but Esther never cried except when she meant it. He sighed again and put his arm around her shoulders.

"It's all right," he said. "They're not going to starve."

"They a-a-a-aren't?" Esther sobbed. "W-w-why aren't they, David?"

"Because we're going to investigate until we find out who really is taking the dogs."

"We are?"

"Sure," David said.

Janie sat up and climbed over Nightmare. "All of us? Are we all going to investigate, David?"

"Look, Janie," he said. "You know what you promised Dad. You know that . . ." He trailed off. There was absolutely no doubt that Janie could cause all sorts of problems, but on the other hand, she did have all that forensic stuff. And he had to admit that she'd always been awfully good at finding out secrets.

"Well look, Janie. If I don't tell on you, and if we let you help out a little, will you promise no more taping Dad's and Molly's friends, or accusing people of murder?"

"Yes, yes. We promise, don't we, Tesser?" Janie jumped to her feet and started bouncing up and down on the bed. Nightmare, who had finally relaxed with his chin on his paws, raised his head and looked at her accusingly. Then he climbed down to the floor and headed for the door. David followed him.

Back in his own room David watched while Nightmare got settled on his lounge chair mattress at the foot of Blair's bed. Blair was already sound asleep, and in a few minutes Nightmare was, too, but David stayed awake for quite a while worrying about the Trans and the missing dogs—and about what he'd gotten himself into by telling Janie he wouldn't rat on her for not giving up on the stolen dogs mystery.

Chapter 10

On Thursday after school was out David went to Wright's Nursery to talk to the Trans. It had been Janie's idea, and she'd made all the arrangements.

"Why should I go to see the Trans?" he'd asked. "If you're right and they're not the ones who've been stealing the dogs, they won't be able to tell me anything I can use in my article."

"Well," Janie said, "you can put in about how people have been blaming them when they're really innocent. And how bad it is for people to blame people for something they haven't done just because some people look a little bit different than other people. You can put that in your story, can't you?"

David laughed. "Wow! That's a whole lot of people for one story. Particularly a story that's supposed to be about dogs."

But Janie kept arguing, and when David finally

agreed and told her to count him in, it was mostly because he was curious about the Trans. He also wanted to find out whether Janie had exaggerated the amount of trouble they were in.

So Janie asked Molly if she could go to the Trans to play with Thuy right after school instead of coming home on the bus. She explained that no one would have to drive into town to pick her up because David, who was riding his bicycle that day, was going to stop by and give her a ride home. Molly checked with David to be sure that he agreed, and then she said okay.

Wright's Nursery took up most of a block on the west side of Steven's Corners. David had been there before. The first time was over two years ago, when he'd come with Dad to look for a replacement for the giant philodendron that had been pushed down the stairs during the Amanda-poltergeist haunting. The other times he'd visited the nursery he'd come with Dad or Molly when they'd been shopping for plants for the garden. He vaguely remembered noticing a house at the rear of the property, beyond the long rows of potted trees; a house that had been lived in by Mr. Wright, the owner of the nursery, until recently, when he built himself a new home on the other side of town. The Tran family had moved in only a few months ago, when Mr. Tran was hired as manager.

When David reached the nursery entrance he parked his bike and walked back past the arbors and greenhouses and through the potted-tree forest and came out in front of a small brown shingle cottage with a wide front porch. Janie and Thuy were sitting on the front steps with their heads close together, whispering to each other. In front of the house Huy and an even smaller kid were playing with a ball.

When Huy saw David he gave the ball to his little brother and stood at attention as David went by, with a you-better-watch-it frown on his face. It was like being threatened by a mouse.

David pretended to be frightened. "Hey, man," he said in a nervous tone of voice, "no ankle biting today, okay? Ankles are out of season."

"Hi David," Janie said, jumping to her feet.

David said, "Hi yourself," and then, "Hi Thuy."

Thuy was as short as Janie and even more wispy and delicate-looking. Standing there side by side on the top step, the two of them looked more than ever like two dolls on a shelf. Janie the blond doll, Dutch maybe, and Thuy the oriental one, with black silk hair and pale golden skin. David grinned. "What's new, dolls?" he said.

They looked at each other and giggled, and then Thuy bent her head so that her long black hair fell forward around her face and said, "Hi David," in a soft whispery voice. Without lifting her eyes she said, "Won't you please come in to see my parents? They would like to meet you."

David was surprised. Janie had told him that Thuy spoke a lot of English, but it was the first time she'd ever said anything to him. He was amazed to hear how little accent she had.

"Sure," he said. "Lead the way."

Afterward David had a hard time describing the Trans and how he felt after his meeting with the whole family. The first time he tried was that evening when he and Amanda were doing their homework in the dining room. David was rewriting his story proposal for Mr. Edmonds's class, and Amanda was doing geometry. The rule was no talking to people who were doing homework, but thinking about the rumors and what they were doing to the Trans made David want to tell someone, and he knew from experience that Amanda never minded being interrupted when she was doing geometry.

"They're . . . well, they're really great people," he told Amanda. "They've been through a lot of stuff, but they don't dwell on it. I mean, they smile a lot, and they try to make you feel comfortable."

"What kind of clothes do they wear? I mean, do they wear sarongs and like that, or do they dress like we do?"

David looked at Amanda. She was wearing her new khaki-colored long johns, only this time they were hanging out from under what looked like a long orange undershirt and a gray vest over that. He grinned.

"Well, I don't think they shop at the Banana Republic, if that's what you mean. But Mrs. Tran was wearing a regular American-type blouse and skirt, and Mr. Tran had on, like, jeans and a work shirt. They're both really good-looking, and the kids are really something—especially the baby."

"They got a real killer baby, huh?" Amanda said.

"Yeah," David said, "yeah." He was remembering how the baby girl had crawled over to his chair and pulled herself up by hanging on to his pants leg and then stood there giving him this really radical smile with only four teeth in it. "Yeah, a real killer," he said. "And the whole family like living here in Steven's Corners a lot, and Mrs. Tran thinks the Wrights' house is practically a mansion, because they had to live in a tent in a refugee camp for a long time before they got to come to America."

"Who told you all that?" Amanda said.

"They did. Their English is pretty good, and when they get stuck they have Thuy explain it. She can say everything in English. But Mr. Tran was the one who told me what Mr. Wright said about selling the nursery and everything."

"Like what?" Amanda said.

"Like Wright said that he'd almost decided to sell the nursery to a land development company once before, and now he was thinking about it again. He didn't exactly say why, I guess, but Mr. Tran said he mentioned the rumors about the stolen dogs. He asked Mr. Tran if he had any idea why people were accusing him and his family. So Mr. Tran thinks that the reason Wright's going to sell out is that he's afraid people who believe the rumors won't buy stuff at the nursery anymore. It looks like it's just as bad as Janie said it was. The Trans didn't say anything about starving to death, but you could tell they're worried."

Amanda slammed her protractor down on the table. "What a nerd!" she said. "That Wright character must be a real wimp, chickening out on the Trans just because of some stupid rumors."

"Yeah, I know," David said.

"Well, what are you going to do about it?"

"Me?" David said. "Well, tomorrow I have to turn in this proposal thing on the story, and if it's okayed, Garvey and I are going to interview the Hardacres—their dog was the first one that got stolen—and we're going to take some pictures and—"

"Yeah, yeah," Amanda said, glaring at David as if it were all his fault. "That's what you're going to do for your assignment, but what are you going to do about the Trans?"

David nodded. He knew what Amanda meant. Unless he got lucky and really found out who'd been stealing the dogs, which wasn't likely, there didn't seem to be much he could do to help.

"Are you going to write about the Trans in your article?" Amanda asked.

"I don't know. I've been thinking about that. Mr. Edmonds said the *Valley Press* was going to print some of the best stories, so if he chooses ours everyone in town might read about it. And unless we had some proof that the Trans are innocent, it might do more harm than good. I mean, I'm afraid all it would do is spread the rumor."

"Yeah, I see what you mean," Amanda said. "Well, what can we do?"

"I don't know." David shook his head slowly. "We just have to find out who the real thief is, I guess. But I sure don't know how."

Amanda stared at him for a minute, spinning her protractor around her finger. Suddenly she slammed it down on the table again and ran out of the room.

"Wow!" David said. You never knew with Amanda, particularly lately. She used to be a lot more consistent. You used to know what she'd be interested in. At first it was supernatural stuff, like seances and poltergeists, and then it was nothing but boys and clothes and rock music and all the latest put-downs. But now you never knew. Lately just when you thought you knew what her reaction would be she'd surprise you by taking an interest in something entirely different—such as other people's problems. He was still wondering about the change when she burst back through the door pulling Janie behind her.

Amanda threw herself back into her chair. "Sit down, Shrimp," she said to Janie. "We have to talk."

Janie looked excited. "What are we doing?" she asked. "Are we having a summit conference?"

"Well, a conference, anyhow," Amanda said. "Somebody has to come up with some good ideas about how to save Mr. Tran's job, and David doesn't seem to have a clue. You're always full of ideas, Shrimp. How about coming up with something?"

Janie bounced with excitement. "Oh, I already have a lot of ideas. One of my ideas is that we ought to offer a reward. Like ten thousand dollars for the person who finds out who's doing it. Or maybe we might—"

"Oh, get real, will you," Amanda said. "Where are you going to get ten thousand dollars? Or even ten dollars, for that matter?"

"Umm." Janie nodded. "I know. But I was thinking we could just say we had the money, and then when we found the thieves we'd be so famous that people would write books about us and put us in the movies and then we'd have plenty of money to pay the reward."

David and Amanda stared at Janie. After a minute she said, "Oh, well, if you don't like that idea I have a lot more. One of my other ideas is to put a tail on the Trans, all of them, and then when the next dog gets stolen we could prove they didn't do it because we could prove they weren't *at* the scene of the crime." Janie looked pleased with herself. "How's that for a good idea?"

"Lousy," David said. "We don't have enough people to tail a whole family at one time."

Just then the kitchen door opened and Esther stuck her head in. She had a milk mustache and her mouth was full. She chewed and swallowed for a minute before she said, "Hi, everybody. Blair and I've been having milk and cookies."

"I never would have guessed," David said.

Esther came into the dining room with Blair right behind her and Nightmare behind Blair. She pulled out a chair and climbed up, while Blair and Nightmare sat down on the floor. "What are you guys doing?" Esther asked.

"We're thinking up good ideas to help the Trans," Janie said. "I just got another one. It's another tailing idea. How about if we put a tail on Mayor Sam and then—"

"Mayor Sam?" David and Amanda said in unison. Amanda looked at David and rolled her eyes and they both started to laugh.

Mayor Sam was the old mutt that hung around downtown in Steven's Corners. He was a big sad-looking dog who was probably part bloodhound and part a lot of other things. Sam didn't have any real owner, but he was something like a town mascot, and he got lots of handouts in the park and from some of the restaurants in the mall. People called him Mayor Sam because a sad-eyed, saggy-jowled man named Sam Spencer had once been the mayor of Steven's Corners.

"A tail on a dog," Amanda said in her most sarcastic tone of voice. "In case you haven't noticed, Shrimp, he already has one."

"A tail on a dog," Esther shrieked as if it were the funniest thing she'd ever heard, and even Blair smiled and whispered into Nightmare's ear, "A tail on a dog, Nightmare. It's a joke."

Janie looked indignant. "It's not a joke. It's a good idea, because the dognappers are probably going to steal him. I'm just surprised they haven't already done it. He'd be just about the easiest dog in town to steal, because he runs loose, even after dark, and that's when all the others were stolen. And if we have a tail on him we'll see them do it, and then the mystery would be solved and we'd know who the real dognappers are."

David and Amanda stopped laughing and looked at each other. Amanda nodded. "You know, the Shrimp just may have something there. Everybody's been so careful lately about keeping their dogs shut up at night, pretty soon Sam will be about the only stealable dog left."

"Yeah," David said. "But how are we going to keep an eye on Mayor Sam? He's usually in the park or hanging around the mall, and we can't hang around there every evening. At least, not on school nights. Dad and Molly would never let us."

"Well, we could do it on Fridays, anyway. You know, because most of the other dogs were stolen on Friday or Saturday evenings. Tomorrow is Friday, and I'll bet we could get permission to go to the mall for a while. Tammy and Eloise hang out there a lot in the evenings, and I bet I could get Mom to let me, if I promise not to stay late. Wouldn't Jeff let you if you told him you were doing research for your English assignment?"

"Well, I don't know. Maybe."

"Us, too?" Janie said. "The twins and I want to help too. Don't we, Esther? Don't we, Blair?"

"Yes, yes," Esther said. "Me too. And Blair too. You want to, don't you, Blair?"

Blair was lying on the floor with his head on Nightmare's shoulder. "What do I want to do?" he asked.

"Watch Mayor Sam so we'll see who tries to steal him."

Blair sat up. "Okay. But I don't think they will."

Janie and Esther suddenly got very quiet. They looked at each other and then back at Blair. "Why don't you think the dognappers will steal Mayor Sam?" Janie asked. "How do you know they won't?"

David knew what was going on. Janie and Esther still believed that Blair had ways of knowing things that nobody else knew. When he was littler he used to tell people that he talked to Harriet, who was maybe the ghost of someone who'd once lived in their house. But now that he was six and had been in school for a while, he learned that talking to someone no one else could see made some people nervous. So he didn't say much about Harriet anymore, but Janie and Esther still thought he talked to her now and then.

"How do you know they won't steal Mayor Sam?" Janie asked again, looking very solemn. "Did someone tell you they wouldn't?"

Blair looked at David and Amanda. Then he looked down and started playing with Nightmare's ear. "I don't remember," he said in a very soft voice. "I don't remember who told me the dognappers don't want Mayor Sam."

Janie and Esther looked at each other and nodded in a significant way. Blair giggled.

"What are you laughing about?" Esther asked.

"They don't want him," Blair said, giggling again, "because he's too ugly."

Everybody laughed and Amanda said, "We're talking about a dognapping, Bleep, not a beauty contest. I'm afraid whoever it was that told you struck out on that one." She turned to David. "Well, what do think? Do you think you could talk your Dad into springing you tomorrow night or what?"

"Yeah, maybe," David said. "It's worth a try."

Janie slid out of her chair and came around to David's. Leaning on his shoulder she said, "And the twins and me? Is it worth a try for you to ask Dad if we can come too?"

"Forget it," David said. "Not a chance."

"Oh," Janie said. "Okay. Come on, twins. Let's go upstairs."

When the kids were gone Amanda grinned at David. "Well, that was easy," she said.

"Yeah," David said. "Maybe too easy."

Chapter 11

Friday was shaping up to be an eventful day. At breakfast David asked if he could spend some time in town that evening, to follow up some leads on his newspaper story, and Dad said yes. And when Amanda asked if she could go along to help, Molly said okay, if she and David were going to be together.

"I don't want you wandering around downtown after dark all by yourself," Molly said.

Amanda grinned. "You mean you want my Great Big Brother to be there to protect me?" she asked. That was all she said, but the way she said it was obviously meant to point out that she had a few inches and several pounds on David, not to mention a better left hook.

David grinned back. "Okay," he said, "so I'm not the Jolly Green Giant. But just wait till next year. I'm catching up."

So the trip into town to check out the Mayor Sam

thing was set up without any complications. Without even any Janie-type complications, which was really hard to believe. In fact, all during the conversation with Dad and Molly, David kept checking on Janie, hoping that she wasn't going to mess things up by trying to get permission to go along. He kept thinking about the un-Janie-like way she'd given up last night when he'd refused to ask permission for her to come. That, and the way her eyes were jittering around like a couple of blue pinwheels, made him suspicious.

Of course, if Janie butted in now and ruined everything David would have only himself to blame for telling her she could help. Expecting the worst at any minute, he finished his third and then his fourth pancake, and Janie went on being unnaturally quiet. When Dad pushed back his chair and left the table she was still sitting there with her eyes jittering and her mouth clamped tightly shut. David could hardly believe his luck.

Friday was also the day that the proposals were due in Mr. Edmonds's class. David handed in the paper because he had rewritten it the night before, but Garvey had done some of the work too. His contribution was a list of old newspaper editions that had stories about previous dog thefts in the area. He'd also written a couple of paragraphs about how they were going to compare the earlier thefts with the recent ones when they finished their investigations. He'd put a lot of effort into it, crossing things out and writing them over two or three times and spelling some words a lot of different ways, to be sure he'd get it right at least once. David's job was to write up the first part of the proposal on Dad's word processor and to include Garvey's stuff in the outline—after making a few changes in the grammar and spelling.

The proposal was just supposed to be a description of the news event they had picked to write about, and an outline of the information they had gathered so far. It was what Mr. Edmonds called a "kick-in-the-pants assignment." A kick-in-the-pants assignment was one that made you get started on a large project so you couldn't put off the whole thing until the last minute.

Mr. Edmonds seemed to like the Garvey-Stanley proposal a lot. He read some parts of it to the class as an example of a good choice of subject for investigative reporting. He said it was good because it would make a story that had a lot of human interest, and because the investigation included live interviews as well as research reading, instead of just one or the other. He gave them an A on the paper.

Since Garvey sat in the front row, where the teacher could keep an eye on him, he was the one who got the paper when Mr. Edmonds handed it back. But from his seat in the third row David was able to get a glimpse of the big red "A" on the front page. He grinned, waiting for Garvey's reaction. It was just possibly the first "A" that Pete Garvey had ever gotten in his whole life. David was certainly expecting some kind of a celebration on Garvey's part. But nothing happened. He turned the paper over and then just sat there staring at the back of it.

David couldn't figure it out. If Ace Maillard or any of Garvey's old buddies had been in the class that might have explained it. In that case it could have been that he was afraid of ruining his anti-everything-to-do-with-school image in front of his pals. But that wasn't it. None of Garvey's old gang was around. Guys like Ace didn't usually take Mr. Edmonds's classes.

But Garvey went right on behaving in an extremely unnatural way. During the whole hour he didn't wise off even once or do anything else to attract attention, and he didn't look back at David at all. By the time the class was dismissed David was beginning to wonder if getting an "A" had been just too much for him, like maybe he'd gone into shock or something.

When the bell rang, Garvey left. Instead of hanging around talking and showing off as he usually did, he grabbed his books and disappeared out the door. Hurrying after him, David practically had to run to catch up.

"Well, Edmonds liked our idea, I guess," David said when he finally caught up, but Garvey only grunted and walked faster. David trotted alongside. After a while he said, "Amanda and I are going to the mall tonight." That will get him, he thought. Nothing in the world could keep Garvey from missing out on a chance to spend the evening with Amanda.

Garvey almost skidded to a stop. "Yeah? Great. What you gonna do? Hang out at Zeke's?" Zeke's was a snack bar where mallies went to meet other mallies.

"No, not really," David said. "We've got a good idea about the stolen-dogs thing. Something we want to follow up on. You want to go?"

Garvey opened his mouth and left it that way for a minute before he clamped it shut. He looked up at the ceiling and then down at his shoes and then back at

David. There was a weird, almost frantic expression on his face. "I dunno," he said. It sounded a lot like a groan. "I dunno. Maybe I can't get out tonight."

What David said was, "Well, suit yourself. I'll let you know what we find out, if anything." But what he was thinking was, Wow! This is serious!

Later, when he told Amanda about Garvey, she didn't say what she was really thinking either—David was pretty sure of that.

They were in the kitchen when he told her, putting the dishes in Molly's new dishwasher, and what Amanda said was, "Well, that's a relief." But then she frowned and after a minute she said, "What'd he mean, he can't get out? I'll bet Garvey hasn't stayed home on a Friday night since he was five years old."

"I know," David said. "I just hope this doesn't mean he's going to quit working on our assignment. I sure don't want to have to start over with a new partner at this point."

"I don't care about your old assignment," Amanda said. "I'm just interested in finding the dog thieves so the Trans will be all right. Come on, put the soap in and let's get going or we won't have time enough to do anything."

David put the soap in the dishwasher, latched the door, and pushed the starter button. But then, of course, Amanda remembered some things she still had to do, like a major remodeling job on her face and hair, so he was still waiting by the front door when Dad came out of the living room with Janie and the twins right behind him.

Oh, oh, David thought. I knew it was too good to be true.

"There you are, David," Dad said. "Glad I caught you. The kids are after me to take them in to see that Disney movie tonight. Could you and Amanda go by the theater at nine forty-five and escort them home on the bus? Save me from making two trips into town. I'll drive all of you in. Just be sure you're at the theater when the first showing lets out. Okay?"

David looked at Janie, and whatever was sinking in the pit of his stomach sank a little further. There was no use protesting, and for all he knew Janie really did plan to see the movie, except something—one of his premonitions perhaps—told him she didn't. But he said okay, and a few minutes later they were all in Dad's station wagon on their way into town. In the back seat the twins were chattering away about the movie they were going to see, but Janie was strangely silent. Sure enough, as soon as Dad dropped them in front of the Roxie and drove off, the truth came out.

"Actually," Janie said. "I've suddenly decided I don't really want to see that movie. I think I'd rather read the book. So the twins can go if they want to, and I'll just go to the mall with you and Amanda. Okay?"

"No," Amanda said. "Why should we take you with us?"

"Well," Janie said, "one reason is that the whole thing was my idea. I was the one who thought of putting a tail on Mayor Sam, remember? So I get to help, or else."

"Or else what, Shrimp?" Amanda said.

"Or else I'll sue. I'll sue for pagerism, like authors do when someone steals their ideas."

"That's plagiarism," David said. "Come on, Amanda. We'd better let her." He knew there wasn't any way to keep Janie from playing detective instead of going to the movie if she'd set her mind on it. If they wouldn't take her with them she'd just sneak off and do it on her own, and no telling how that would end up.

"Okay, okay," Amanda said. "I give up."

"Great," Janie said, and started off toward the mall.

"I want to help put a tail on Mayor Sam too," Esther said.

"You mean you're going to miss this wonderful movie?" Amanda winked at David. "I hear it's very good."

"I hear it's scary," Esther said. "Blair and I don't want to see a scary movie all by ourselves. Do we, Blair?"

Blair, who had been busy checking out the movie poster, hadn't been listening.

"Do we, Blair?" Esther said again, louder.

"What?" Blair said. "Do we what?"

"Want to see the movie."

Blair nodded. "Yes, we want to see it. Don't we?"

"No, we don't!" Esther yelled. Then she grabbed Blair and whispered in his ear.

Blair listened, nodding his head and rolling his big spacy eyes. When Esther turned him loose and ran off after Janie, Blair went on nodding thoughtfully. Then he smiled apologetically at David and Amanda. "No, we don't," he said. "We want to pin a tail on Mayor Sam." Then he ran after Janie and Esther.

"Arghh," Amanda said in a half-strangled tone of voice. When David looked at her she did a silent scream number and pretended to be pulling her hair out with both hands. "Arghh!" she said again. "That did it. They pushed me too far this time. I think I'm permanently brain damaged." She crossed her eyes, let her tongue loll out, and staggered around in circles.

David laughed. "Knock it off," he said. "You'll get us arrested. Come on. We'd better catch up with them."

They started off at a fast walk, but the little kids were still almost a block ahead when David became aware of the sound of a racing motor. He looked back and saw the street rod, and then ahead to where Janie and the twins were just stepping off the curb a half block away. He was already running as he yelled, "Look out!" but the car shot past him long before he reached the corner.

Blair, who was out ahead, was already in the street. He stopped when David yelled, looked around, and seemed to freeze, with the car only a few yards away. David was running at top speed, but he could never have reached Blair in time. But Janie did. Reaching out, she jerked him back just as the street rod roared past. When David got to the corner all three kids were staring bug-eyed after the rapidly disappearing car.

"He almost hit Blair." Janie's voice was a shaky whisper.

David had to swallow hard before he could answer. "I know," he said. And then because the crazy idiots in the car weren't around to yell at, he started yelling at the kids, bawling them out for running ahead and being careless about street crossings.

Then Amanda caught up and she started yelling too. But what she was yelling were some comments about the driver of the car. Janie and the twins seemed to be much more interested in what she was yelling than what David was. When she finally ran down, Janie said, "I said just one of those words in class last year and Mrs. Majors made me stay after school for a week."

That seemed to calm Amanda down a little, and after she'd taken a few deep breaths she asked David if he thought the car was Mack Maillard's.

"I'm not sure," David said. "It might have been. But there's this other guy named Potter who has one a lot like Mack's. It might have been his."

"Well, whoever he is he's a real . . ." Janie and the twins were staring at Amanda expectantly, and she stopped and shrugged and then went on. "Come on. What are we standing around here for? We've got things to do."

They all crossed the street very carefully and started down Main to the mall, but Blair kept lagging behind. Every few feet he stopped and stared off down to where the street rod had disappeared where Main Street curved around Muir Park.

"Come on, we have to hurry," David said the third time he had to drop back to get Blair going again. "What is it? What's the matter?" Actually, he knew what the matter was, or at least he thought he did. Coming that close to being run over was enough to space anyone out. But Blair wasn't looking scared or even worried, just thoughtful. "What's the matter, Blair?" David asked again.

"Those guys in that car . . ." Blair paused, and then he nodded. "They're going to do something bad. Something real bad."

"Tell me about it," David said. "They're going to kill somebody someday if they keep driving like that."

"And dogs," Blair said. "Are they going to hurt dogs, too, David?"

"Right. Dogs and people and chickens and anything else that gets in their way. Now come on. We've got things to do." And he gave Blair a push to get him moving.

When they got to the main entrance of the mall, big double doors leading into the covered walkway between the two long rows of shops, they stopped and looked around. There was no sign of Sam.

"Well," Amanda said, "he's not here, so if they haven't nabbed him already he's either in the park or inside the mall."

Amanda was probably right. People said that Sam had a sleeping place in the park under the bandstand, but he loved the mall and he was usually inside it or waiting at the entrance to be let in. A few of the shop owners—the ones the mallies called Sam Bouncers—kept putting him out again, but some of the other owners—the Sam Boosters—and all of the mallies kept letting him back in. Sam had gotten smart about telling the Bouncers from the Boosters, and he was good at doing a disappearing act when a Bouncer showed up.

"Okay," David said, "here's the drill. You little kids stay right here just inside the doors, and keep your eyes open. Amanda and I will cruise down the mall to see if he's already inside. If he shows up at the door you guys come and get us. Okay?"

The little kids agreed, so Amanda and David started off down the mall, one on each side, looking behind the big planters and into all the open shops. Amanda stopped two or three times to say hi to some of her mallie friends but she didn't slow things down too much, and they were almost at the entrance of Sears when Esther came trotting up on her short legs, all out of breath.

"David," she gasped, "come on. We saw Sam. He came to the door."

Grabbing Esther's hands, David and Amanda pulled her along between them as they ran back up the mall, dodging mallies and shoppers and swinging Esther right over the top of some of the smaller planting boxes. But when they got to the entrance there was no sign of Sam—or of Janie and Blair.

Outside the doors they looked both ways, up and down Main Street.

"They're gone," David said. "Maybe they're back in the mall. Maybe we ran right past them."

"I—I don't think so," Esther said. "I think they went to the park. Sam came out of Bill's Barbecue with a great big bone and somebody let him out and he started right off toward the park. We tried to stop him but he wouldn't, and that's when Janie told me to get you guys. Janie said she and Blair were going to tail Sam."

David turned to stare down the two blocks to where Main Street curved around the dark shadowy bulk of Muir Park. It was completely dark now, and in the park only a few streetlamps made islands of light in a sea of darkness.

"I knew it," he said, and began to run.

Chapter 12

They ran all the way to the park. Between them, hanging on to their hands, Esther skimmed over the pavement, her short chubby legs flying, her feet hardly touching the ground. When they stopped just inside the stone pillars that marked the park's main entrance she was breathless with excitement.

"That was fun," she said. "Let's run some more."

"Shhh!" David was staring down toward the fountain and on past it in the direction of the playground. Nothing moved. The entire park seemed deserted. The air was damp and heavy, and drifting wisps of fog turned the widely spaced lamps into hazy halos. The park's winding pathways had become narrow tunnels of misty light dwindling away into darkness.

"David"—Esther's voice was whiny—"what's the matter? Why can't we run some more?" Then, suddenly worried, "Where are they? Where are Janie and Blair?"

"Good question," Amanda said.

David glanced at her. She was staring into the darkness, squinty-eyed and frowning. Turning to David, she went on frowning, accusingly. "Okay, mastermind. What do we do now?"

"Look," he said. "I told them to stay in the mall. It's not my fault."

"Yes it is. She's your sister."

"That's not exactly my fault either," David said. "I didn't pick her out, you know. I don't know why—" He had been going to say something about the way Amanda always handled a crisis by blaming somebody, but fortunately he caught himself. There was no time to waste arguing.

"Come on," he said instead. "Lets go." Turning to the right, toward a smaller, even dimmer path that wound through a grove of redwoods, he pulled Esther after him.

Amanda stayed where she was, still holding on to Esther's left hand. When David's forward progress jerked Esther to the right, Amanda jerked her back— and hard.

"I don't want to go that way," she said. "It's too dark. Let's go this way."

"Come on," David said, pulling harder. "The bandstand is this way. We have to go to the bandstand."

"Ouch!" Esther squealed. "You're stretching me."

They turned loose and she plopped herself down on the ground and rubbed her shoulders. "You nerds," she said. "That hurt."

"I'm sorry, Tesser," David said. "But we have to find Janie and Blair. And they're probably at the bandstand, because that's where Mayor Sam has his hideout, so that's probably where he was taking the bone." He looked at Amanda. "Don't you think so?"

Amanda glared at him for a moment before she said, "Yeah, I guess you're right. So come on. Let's get going. But I *don't like it.*" She said it again as they started off, and she kept on saying it under her breath as they made their way through the darkness of the grove. "I don't like it. I don't like it."

David led the way. Under the tall trees the air was moist and still and heavy with fog. A thick carpet of redwood needles hushed their footsteps, and except for the distant hum of traffic there was no sound at all. Between the widely spaced lampposts the darkness was almost complete. David moved slowly, feeling his way with his feet and keeping his eyes on the misty glow of the next lamp. He had been shuffling forward for what seemed a long time when a hand grabbed his shoulder and jerked him to a stop. "Shh! Listen," Amanda whispered in his ear. "Did you hear that?"

"What?"

"Shh. *Listen.*"

David listened. Except for a horn honking a long way away and Amanda's heavy breathing in his ear, he could hear nothing at all. "I don't hear anything," he whispered. "What did it sound like?"

"Like footsteps. Over there, under the trees."

"I heard it." Esther tugged at David's shirt. "I heard it. David, I'm scared."

"Shh." David leaned forward, away from Amanda's noisy breathing, and then he heard it too. Someone was walking slowly and carefully through the darkness under the trees. *Step, step, step,* and then a pause. And then the sound again. *Step. Step. Step.*

Fear crawled up the back of David's neck like a large spider. "Come on. Keep walking." His voice came out thin and narrow through his tightened throat as he moved forward, with Esther hanging on to his hand on one side and Amanda gripping his arm on the other.

Under the next lamppost they paused again, and again they heard the footsteps, but more distant now, holding back, lurking in the darkness. David moved on quickly, and as they rounded the next curve in the path they came out into the clearing around the bandstand.

Out here in the open there was more light, and the fog seemed less heavy. The bandstand, an octagonal structure that looked like an oversize Victorian gazebo, glowed a ghostly white in the hazy light. And up on its raised platform . . . something was moving. Something round and head-shaped came slowly up over the railing and then disappeared again in an instant. But even in that brief glimpse David was sure he recognized the tangle of curly blond hair. It had to be Janie.

Forgetting about everything else, even the following footsteps, he began to run, pulling Esther after him. But Amanda ran faster, and when he reached the steps leading up to the stage she was ahead of him. As he was dragging Esther up the last few steps he heard Janie say, "Shhh! Don't make so much noise, and get *down.* You'll ruin everything."

Janie was tugging at Amanda, trying to make her crouch down behind the railing.

Amanda pushed her away. "What's going on? Let go, Shrimp. What do you think you're doing?"

"We have to keep out of sight," Janie whispered, "or he'll start all over again."

Amanda went down on her knees behind the railing and Janie grabbed David. "You too, David. Get down. And Tesser, go over there beside Blair."

David squatted down, but he held on to Janie and pulled her over beside him. "Okay," he said. "Tell me. What's going on? What are you up to?"

"We're tailing Mayor Sam." Janie sounded surprised that he should ask. "He's burying his bone right now, but when he gets through he'll probably go back to the mall. And I've deduced that that's when the dognappers will probably strike. Let's see. Maybe he's finished." She took hold of the railing and cautiously raised herself up until her eyes were barely above the rim. "See. There he is. Still digging."

David, and next to him Amanda, and then Esther and Blair followed Janie's example and peered out over the rim of the railing. There in the clearing, only a few yards away, Mayor Sam was industriously digging a hole.

Sam was a long, low dog with loose floppy skin. He was fairly funny-looking even when he wasn't doing anything special; digging a hole he was pretty ridiculous. Balancing on his hind legs, he brought up dirt with both front feet and sprayed it out behind him, nearly tying himself into a knot at every stroke. Somebody, probably Esther, giggled, and David himself barely managed to stifle a snicker.

Sam dug for several seconds, walked around the hole sniffing at it, and then dug some more. After he'd inspected his work once more he trotted away a few feet, picked up a huge bone, and trotted back. Leaning over the hole he dropped the bone in. and then stopped. Slowly and cautiously, with his long head hung low, he turned to look at the bandstand.

"Shhh," Janie hissed. "Get down."

The row of watchers dropped down out of sight all at once, like the target ducks in a shooting booth at the fair. But apparently they weren't quick enough. A moment later when David carefully peered back over the railing, Mayor Sam was getting his bone out of the hole.

"Phooey!" Janie whispered. "He saw us. Now he'll dig a whole new hole. This is the third one."

Sure enough, Sam was beginning all over again in a new spot a little farther from the bandstand. This time everybody stayed down out of sight, sitting in a row with their backs to the railing. Now and then David pulled the hood of his jacket almost over his face as camouflage and carefully peered over the edge just long enough to be sure that Sam was still there. Then he sat back down and waited with the others.

With nothing to do but wait, there was time to think. David thought briefly of the footsteps they had heard in the grove and decided it had been their imagination, or maybe something natural, like a large raccoon. He also thought things like Why in the everloving blue-eyed world am I sitting on the cold damp floor of a bandstand in the middle of a deserted park waiting for a silly-looking dog to finish burying a bone? And then he told himself, You know why you're here; it's what you get for weakening and telling Janie she could help. You'd think you'd learn, Stanley, but you never do!

Before long everyone was squirming, and Esther was

complaining that she was cold by poking David and pantomiming violent shivers. David was fed up. There was no guarantee that Sam was going to go back to the mall when he finished hiding his bone, and there was even less reason to think that the dognappers would pick tonight to try to grab him if he did. David had had his doubts about the whole Tailing Mayor Sam operation from the beginning. And now, seen from the cold, damp bandstand floor, the whole thing was beginning to seem like one of those dreams where you keep doing stupid things that you know are stupid but you can't seem to stop.

He would check on Sam one more time, he decided, and if the dog was still fooling around with his bone, that was it, they were all leaving. The kids, too, whether they wanted to or not. Pulling his hood almost across his face he peered out—just in time to see Sam drop the bone into the hole and, after another careful look around, start to cover it up. He stopped and inspected and dug again several times before he was satisfied, but at last he turned away and started across the clearing in the direction of the mall. The path he was taking would bring him close to the bandstand.

"He's leaving," David whispered. "Get down everyone, and be still."

Everyone crouched low behind the railing. David was still on his hands and knees, head low, when he became aware of a sound. It was a huffing, scratching, thumping noise, and it got louder and louder and then something licked his ear.

"Hi, Mayor Sam," Blair said.

Floppy ears flying, Sam bounded over to Blair,

pushed him over, and licked his face. He always did that when he saw Blair. All dogs were crazy about Blair, and Mayor Sam was crazier than most. Blair giggled and squirmed, trying to cover his face, and then Esther got into the act. Grabbing Sam around the neck, she tried to pull him away. In a minute there was a kind of three-way dog-wrestling match going on in the middle of the bandstand floor.

"Twins," Janie said. "Stop that this minute. How are we going to tail Sam now? You're spoiling everything. David. Make them stop."

David was bending over the tangle of kids and dog, telling them to knock it off, when the sound of heavy footsteps on the bandstand steps made him whirl around. Someone was standing at the top of the stairs. It was a man, a man wearing dark bulky clothing and a cap with earflaps. In the dim light the eyes seemed to be blank black holes and his face seemed fur-trimmed, like the face of a werewolf.

"All right!" The voice was loud and harsh. "What's going on here? Turn loose of that dog."

Blair and Esther scrambled to their feet. David's heart was still pounding, but his breath was beginning to come back. He could see now that the man's eyes were just deep-set, and it was his cap's earflaps and not his cheeks that were fur-trimmed.

The stranger pulled a flashlight out from under his heavy jacket and began to shine it around. When he got to David he stopped. "Okay," he said. "Do you want to tell me what's going on here?"

"All right," David said, blinking in the glare of the

powerful flashlight. "Okay. We were just . . ." He hesitated. "Do you mind telling us who you are, sir?"

"Police," the man said curtly. "Officer Wilmot. Steven's Corners Police Department. Now get on with it. What are you kids up to?"

Janie tugged at David's sleeve. "His badge," she said. "Make him show you his badge."

David looked at Janie and then back into the flashlight's glare. "Sir . . ." he said.

A hand reached out from behind the blinding light, holding a thin wallet with a shiny silver badge fastened to it.

"Okay," the harsh voice said. "Now get on with it. Let's hear your story."

"Well . . ." David said slowly, trying to decide where to start. If he began at the very beginning, with Janie's detective agency and the Trans' problem and the assignment for Mr. Edmonds's class, it would take forever, and the officer would never believe it anyway. So he decided just to tell a small part of it. "Well," he said, "my name is David Stanley, and these kids are my brother and sisters, and we were all at the mall this evening, only Janie and Blair here came over to the park and so we followed them and—"

"Okay, okay." The officer sounded angry and impatient. "But what were you doing up here on the bandstand? Come here, kid."

He stepped closer, and with his free hand he began patting David's jacket. David was wearing his down-filled ski jacket and it was pretty bulky and lumpy and the policeman patted quite a while before he seemed satisfied. Then he turned the flashlight's beam toward Amanda.

"Okay, you next," he said, but as he moved toward Amanda he almost stepped on Janie. Holding her jacket open Janie said, "You can search me next, Mr. Officer. I'm not armed. I don't have a gun or anything, Mr. Officer."

The policeman brought the beam of his flashlight down, way down, to Janie's face. "Well, well," he said. "I'm glad to hear you're not armed, young lady. But I wasn't really looking for weapons."

"You weren't?" Janie sounded amazed. "What were you looking for then?"

"Spray cans." The light moved around again picking out faces. "Any of you kids got a spray paint can?" The voice was harsh and grating again.

Of course they all said no, but the officer didn't seem to believe them. Stopping with the light on Blair, the policeman moved forward and bent down. "You look like a boy who'd tell the truth," he said. "Any of you kids been spraying stuff on benches and in the rest rooms?"

Spotlighted by the beam of the flashlight, Blair's big spacy eyes and halo of blond curls were almost unreal. "No," he said in his soft whispery voice. "We weren't spraying things. We don't have any spray cans."

Blair stopped talking, but the officer went on looking at him for a minute or so, not saying anything. He just stayed in the same bent-over position, staring at Blair as if he were hypnotized. Blair did that to people sometimes. At last the officer kind of pulled himself together and asked in a more normal-sounding tone of voice,

"Then what were you doing here in the park at this time of night?"

"We were following Mayor Sam," Blair said. He bent over and patted Sam, who had flopped down beside his feet. "We were just following this doggie."

The officer shone the light on Sam. "Why, that's the stray that hangs out around town," he said. "Why were you following him?"

No one volunteered to answer. David was trying to think of a simple and believable way to explain it when the policeman said, "Wait a minute! How many other dogs you kids been 'following' lately? Here I thought I'd just caught a few spray paint vandals and it looks like maybe I got me some dog thieves. Okay, come on, kids. We're going to the station."

Chapter 13

The police station in Steven's Corners was in the old part of town, next to the courthouse and just in front of the jail. When the black and white patrol car entered Courthouse Square, it turned to the left and went around to a side entrance. David was glad of that. All the way from the park he'd been flashing on the whole Stanley family being herded out of the back seat of a police car right in the middle of Courthouse Square. It was the kind of thing you hardly ever had to think about, except in a nightmare. So when the car turned in between buildings and stopped behind a high fence, he breathed a sigh of relief.

"Whew," he said, "glad we're getting out back here." He said it mostly to Amanda. Amanda had been quiet, not only in the patrol car but also before that, in the park. David wanted—well, not really to cheer her up;

he didn't suppose that was possible, under the circumstances—but just to get her talking again.

But Amanda didn't seem to hear. She just went on staring straight ahead with her mouth set in a straight line and a squinty look around her eyes.

"Where? Where are we getting out?" Janie said. Janie was in the middle, wedged in between David with Esther on his lap and Amanda with Blair on hers. "Where are we getting out? Let me see. David, is this the police station?"

David sighed. Janie, on the other hand, had been talking constantly. She'd talked all the way through the park and down Pine Street to the corner where the officer had left his car. She'd asked Officer Wilmot if he'd been in the park on a stakeout, and what words had been sprayed on the benches, and if the police had caught any spray painters yet, and a whole lot more. And then, after he'd put them all in the back seat of the patrol car, she'd knocked on the window between the two seats and asked him if the glass was bulletproof.

As soon as Janie had pulled herself up to her feet she said, "Yes, it is. Look! It's the police station," in the tone of voice most kids would use to say "Look, it's Disneyland." Then she started tromping all over David as she tried to get to the door.

"Sit down, Janie!" David said. "The door won't open from the inside. Wait till he opens it."

But Janie had to try it for herself. Standing on David's right foot, she tried the handle several times. "You're right," she said. "It won't. I guess that's so desperate criminals can't jump out and escape. That's a good idea, isn't it?"

The minute Officer Wilmot opened the door, Janie jumped out, using David's instep as a springboard. And as David lifted Esther to the ground and climbed out himself, he heard her say, "That's a good idea, Officer Wilmot. I mean, having the doors so they won't open from the inside. Do you have to unlock them with a key, or do you have a switch up by the steering wheel?"

"Both," Wilmot said in a fed-up tone of voice. "Works either way." His voice was still harsh and grating, but now, under a bright floodlight and without his cap, he didn't look nearly so much like a werewolf. He still looked squarish and bulky, but David was surprised to notice that he actually was fairly short—in fact, not a whole lot taller than Amanda. And his frown, which had looked so ferocious in the dim light of the park, now just seemed bothered and irritable.

Janie was teetering around on her tiptoes the way she usually did when she was excited, and Wilmot reached out and grabbed her by the wrist and held her while he watched the rest of the kids climb out of the car.

"Stand still a minute, can't you?" he said. "And the rest of you line up over here. Single file."

"With our hands over our heads?" Janie asked, holding her free arm up in the air. "Put your hands up, twins. See, like this."

"That's not necessary," Wilmot said, but Janie was so busy telling the twins what to do that she didn't hear him, and the twins didn't either, so when they all trooped into the station the three little kids still had their hands in the air.

Inside the police station there was a waiting area with benches around the walls and then, behind a railing, a lot of desks and file cabinets. Several people were standing by the file cabinets and a few more were at the desks, and they all turned around to watch as the Stanleys and Officer Wilmot entered. Some of them started grinning.

"Hey, Wilmot," somebody said. "What you got there? The midget Mafia?"

Officer Wilmot didn't answer. He just opened a gate in the railing and led the way across the room, ignoring the grins and remarks of the other officers. Watching him, the way he kind of strutted with his chin stuck out and a superserious expression on his face, David was beginning to get the picture.

Great, he thought. Just my luck. Just my luck to get arrested by a someone who has something to prove— like maybe who's a supercop and who isn't.

When Officer Wilmot got to his desk he sat down and got out a bunch of notebooks and started asking questions. First he took all their names and ages.

He started with David. "Okay, kid, what's your full name?" he said. It wasn't until David started to tell him that he looked up and saw that Janie and the twins still had their hands up over their heads. He was telling them again to put their hands down, when another man, a tall lanky guy with dark curly hair, came over carrying some handcuffs.

"Need a little help here, Ernie?" he said to Officer Wilmot. "You must need some extra cuffs with a mob like this on your hands." He squatted down in front of Blair and snapped the cuffs over his wrists. For a minute David felt angry. From the look on the curly-headed guy's face it seemed as if he was probably trying to be funny, but handcuffing a little kid like Blair was a dumb joke. It might really scare him.

But David needn't have worried. Blair got the joke. He waited until the curly-headed guy stood up and then he put his arms straight down and the handcuffs slipped right over his hands and fell onto the floor with a loud clatter. Blair and the tall guy grinned at each other, and some other people laughed out loud.

"Butt out, Donnelly," Officer Wilmot said. "I got everything under control here."

"I wouldn't be too sure." Donnelly, the curly-headed policeman, was looking serious, except for around his eyes. "Looks like a pretty dangerous bunch to me. Think I'd better hang around to back you up." He sat down on the edge of the next desk.

Wilmot turned to Amanda and asked her her name, and when she said it was Amanda Randall he got all confused. It took him a while to understand that even though they were all part of the same family, Amanda had a different last name because she was their stepsister. He seemed to blame his confusion on her, and he started speaking to her in a stern and disapproving tone of voice. David could have told him that was the wrong approach to take with Amanda.

By then she'd lost her pale, tense look and had begun to smile her upside-down smile. David was glad to see her looking more like herself, but at the same time that expression had always made him a little nervous.

"*Step*sister?" Amanda's voice was sarcastically patient. "You've heard of stepsisters, haven't you? Like in Cinderella?"

Wilmot looked up suspiciously. "No need to get

smarty, young lady," he said. David winced. Amanda looked at David and rolled her eyes with a can-you-believe-this-guy expression, and her smile got even more dangerous.

"All right," Officer Wilmot said. "Why were you following the dog in question?"

"The dog in question?" Amanda said. "I must have missed something. Was there a question with a dog in it?"

Somebody snickered and Wilmot glared. "Why," he said clearly and distinctly, "did you follow the dog called Mayor Sam into the park?"

"I didn't," Amanda said even more clearly and distinctly. "I followed Janie and Blair into the park."

Things were definitely not going well. "Er, excuse me," David broke in. "See, we were all at the mall together, only after we'd been there a little while Janie and Blair went off after Mayor Sam. And so we had to go looking for them. We'd just found them in the park when you came along and arrested us."

Somebody, probably the Donnelly guy, snickered. Officer Wilmot glared at David and told him not to interrupt, but then he started writing down a bunch of stuff and when he'd finished he didn't ask Amanda any more questions. Instead he went on to Janie, and that's when things really fell apart.

Janie insisted on telling him not only how old she was but also what her IQ was and that she didn't think she had a rap sheet but that if she did she wanted to know what was on it.

"I guess I'll have one now for sure," she said. "I guess we all will. Are we going to be mugged and fingerprinted? And take lie detector tests? Are you going to make us take lie detector tests? I don't mind. I've always wanted to take one. And when you give Esther her test, would you mind asking her an extra question? Would you just ask her who ate my chocolate Santa Claus?" She ran around the desk and whispered loudly in Officer Wilmot's ear, "I know she did it but she keeps saying she didn't."

By this time most of the officers in the station—two men in uniform and three or four men and women who weren't, and a meter maid—had edged over to where they could hear what was going on. And every time Janie said anything they'd all grin and punch each other. They all—all, that is, except Officer Wilmot— seemed to be enjoying themselves. To his surprise David found that he was beginning to enjoy himself too. What he was enjoying was watching somebody else trying to cope with Amanda and Janie, and making a mess of it.

"Okay, okay!" Officer Wilmot snapped, sounding even more irritated. "You just go back over there and sit down. I want to talk to your brother." He motioned toward Blair and said, "Come over here, kid."

Janie started off, but then she stopped and leaned over the desk. "You spelled 'Stanley' wrong," she said pointing at the page. "There's an 'e' before the 'y.' Oh, and something else; you haven't read us our rights yet. Aren't you supposed to read us our rights?" She turned to the twins. "He's supposed to tell us about how we don't have to answer any questions until we've talked to our lawyers. Don't tell him anything until he reads you your rights."

David heard some half smothered choking noises and turned around. The other officers were trying not to laugh, only some of them weren't trying very hard. Officer Donnelly, in fact, was laughing right out loud. And the more they laughed the more angry Officer Wilmot looked. But suddenly everything got a lot quieter. The door to a glassed-in room at the other end of the station opened, and a man came toward Officer Wilmot's desk. He was a middle-aged man with broad shoulders and a big square face. David guessed that he was the captain or sheriff or something like that.

"All right," the new man said. "What's going on here?"

"Sir"—Officer Wilmot got to his feet—"I picked up these kids in the park. I was out there on the spray paint vandal detail and I found this bunch up on the bandstand near where a lot of spray paint vandalism was perpetrated last weekend, if you recall, sir. And then—"

"Any evidence?" the new guy interrupted. "Did they have spray paint cans on them?"

"Well, no sir. But when I interrogated them the smallest boy there admitted that they'd come into the park following a dog. It was that mutt that hangs around the mall a lot. Sam, they call him. But anyway, they had this dog up on the bandstand with them when I caught up with them. And just as I came on the scene they were struggling with the animal." Officer Wilmot was looking pleased with himself. "Trying to get a rope or something on him, I imagine. And I just thought, sir, in light of the stolen dog situation here in town, that it might be a good idea to bring them in."

The new man was listening with a funny kind of frown on his face, and when Wilmot finally stopped talking the captain—it turned out that he was the captain, just as David thought—said, "Okay, who wants to tell me what you kids were doing in the park with Mayor Sam?" He looked around and then said to Amanda, "How about you? You look like you might be the oldest."

Amanda shrugged. "Okay. But it wasn't my idea. None of it was my idea. I was just trying to help David on his assignment."

"Assignment?" The captain looked at David.

"Yes sir," David said. "In my English class—I'm at Wilson Junior High—and we've been studying about how to write news stories, and I have to write about a local event of some kind. So I decided to—"

"Actually, it was my idea," Janie said. "May I tell about it?"

The captain turned and looked down at Janie. David saw his lips twitch a little, but then he got a serious look on his face. "So, it was all your idea, was it? Does that mean you're the brains of this outfit?"

"Well, I wouldn't exactly say that"—Janie was trying to look modest but it wasn't coming off very well—"but I'd been checking out the MO of the dog-stealing perps and—"

"Just a minute." The captain was still trying to look serious but the corners of his mouth kept twitching. "The MO of the perps, you say?"

"Right." Janie said. "MO. That means 'method of operation,' and perps . . ." She trailed off. "You know what all that stuff means."

"Right," the captain said. "I just wondered if you did."

"Of course I do. 'Perps' is for 'perpetrators.' You know: the guys who did it. The guys who did it are the perps."

More people were laughing, but when the captain turned around they quieted down. He turned back to Janie. "Okay," he said. "I think there's a little bit too much kibitzing going on here. I want you and Blair here to come into my office with me and we'll have a little chat in private."

Esther looked crushed. "And me too?" she said in a whiny tone of voice. "I want to go too."

"Sure, you come along too," the captain said. "But I think we can do without your big brother and sister for the time being. We'll leave them here with Officer Wilmot for now."

So the captain went off with the three little kids and after they were gone Wilmot asked a few more dumb questions and then he told David and Amanda go out to the waiting area beyond the railing. The police officers drifted off to their own desks. David and Amanda were left sitting on the bench by the front door.

David grinned weakly at Amanda and said, "I guess they don't think we're going to make a run for it."

"What?" Amanda's smile was sarcastic. "And leave the brains of the outfit behind?"

After a while David discovered that when he stood up he could check out what was going on in the captain's office through the glass wall. The captain was sitting in a chair, and he had all three of the kids sitting along the edge of his desk. David could tell which one of the kids was talking by watching the captain's eyes. Most of the time it was Janie, but Blair talked some and so did Esther.

"Look," David said to Amanda, and she stood up and watched for a while too. After a minute or two she said, "Oh man! What do you think she's telling him?"

"I haven't a clue," David said.

"Well, you ought to. She's your sister."

David sighed. "I keep telling you. It's not my fault."

Chapter 14

Whatever it was that Janie was telling the police captain must not have been incriminating, because when he finally came out of his office with the three little kids he said he was releasing everybody, all five of them, immediately.

"You are?" Janie looked surprised and a little bit disappointed. "Aren't you even going to fingerprint us first? I was hoping you were going to fingerprint us."

"No, I don't think think that will be necessary," the captain said.

Officer Donnelly had come over to the railing and was listening.

Janie sighed. "No fingerprints," she told the twins.

"Just wait here a minute," the captain said. "I'll be right back." Then he went across the station and started talking to Officer Wilmot.

"Nope, no fingerprints this time," Officer Donnelly

said. "This time we're just going to let you off with a warning."

"Oh, okay," Janie said. "What's the warning?"

Officer Donnelly looked over his shoulder toward where the captain was talking to Wilmot. Then he lowered his voice and said, "The warning is, stay away from Officer Wilmot when he's in a bad mood."

"Okay," Janie whispered back. "How can we tell if he's in a bad mood?"

Donnelly cupped his mouth with both hands. "If he's awake. If he's awake he's in a bad mood."

Officer Donnelly's phone rang then and he went off to answer it. Amanda grabbed Janie by the shoulder. "What did you say in there? What were you telling that dude when you were sitting on his desk?"

"Oh, we were just sharing our clues with Captain Lowell," Janie said. "We told him all about our investigations, and he taped it all down on a big tape recorder. He said it would be very useful. We told him all about Mrs. Ferris and the Boggses and why we think the dognappers are going to try to get Mayor Sam next and then—"

"I didn't," Blair said. He poked Janie in the ribs and went on poking her. "I didn't, Janie."

"You didn't what?" David asked.

Janie pushed Blair's finger away and said, "Oh, Blair doesn't think the dognappers are going to steal Mayor Sam."

"Oh, yeah. I remember," David grinned. "Because he's too ugly. Wasn't that what you said, Blair?"

Blair nodded. "And old, maybe. Maybe those bad

guys don't like ugly old dogs." Blair thought for a moment and then said, "I do. I like ugly old dogs."

"You like any kind of dog," David said, and then he asked Janie what made the captain decide to let them all go. But before she could answer, the captain came over and said that Officer Wilmot was going to drive them back to the mall. David didn't think that was necessary, but the captain insisted. "Officer Wilmot will take you," he said. "Under the circumstances it's the least he can do."

The captain didn't explain exactly what he meant by that, but it was pretty obvious that he didn't think that Officer Wilmot's big arrest was such a hot idea. The captain told them all good-bye and shook their hands, and most of the other police officers crowded around the railing and said good-bye too. One of the women officers got out a box of chocolate-covered cherries and gave everybody one—except Esther, who somehow managed to get three. The tall policeman named Donnelly shook hands, too, and said to be sure and let him know if they got any more leads on the dognappers, and to remember the warning.

With all the candy-passing and good-byes it was quite a while before they got going, and when they finally reached the parking lot Officer Wilmot was already waiting in his patrol car. They'd just gotten into the back seat when Janie began looking frantically through the pockets of her coat and saying, "My clue book. My clue notebook. It's gone. I must have left it in the captain's office."

Janie's clue book was a small spiral notebook that she carried around everywhere, and David knew there wasn't any use trying to get her to leave without it. He also knew that if she went back into the police station to look for it, she might start talking and be gone for hours. So David asked Officer Wilmot to wait a minute while he went himself.

Wilmot glared at David and said, "Okay, but step on it. I've got better things to do than chauffeur a bunch of kids around."

Amanda pointed at Wilmot with her pointing finger hidden behind her other hand, "Watch out," she whispered. "I think he's awake." Then she and Janie giggled.

When David walked into the police station he thought for a minute that all the police officers had been called away on a big emergency, because the whole office seemed to be empty. But then he heard a muffled noise in the direction of the captain's office, and there they all were. All the officers, and the meter maid, too, were crowded around the captain's desk, and they were all laughing their heads off.

No one noticed him, so he finally went through the railing and right over to the glass door. From there he could see that the captain was running a tape deck and they were all listening and laughing like a bunch of hyenas. When David knocked on the door it suddenly got quiet and the captain turned off the tape. Then he came out and David told him about the missing notebook.

They found Janie's clue book under the desk, and then the officers said good-bye to David again. They were all extra friendly and helpful, but some of them kept grinning and making little smothered snorting noises. And just as David was going out the door he heard them start laughing again.

On the way home David kept grinning himself, thinking about it. Janie could be pretty funny all right, when she wasn't driving you up the wall, and he could see how all her private investigator ideas must have seemed like a riot to the police officers. Later that evening David told Amanda about what he'd seen when he went back into the police station.

"I guess it could have been something else they were listening to, but I'll bet it was the tape the captain made of Janie."

Amanda shrugged. "Yeah," she said. "Sure it was. That Janie's a real riot. Are you going to tell her about it?"

"I haven't decided for sure. But I don't think I will." What he'd been thinking was that Janie might be embarrassed at being laughed at when she hadn't been trying to be funny.

"Right!" Amanda said. "Don't tell her. The little nerd already thinks she's Princess Di."

"You mean you think she'd like it?" David asked.

"She'd love it," Amanda said.

On second thought, David decided, Amanda was probably right.

The next morning when David came down to the kitchen Dad and Molly were already at the table. They'd been listening to the news on the radio, and when David came in they told him that there'd been another stolen dog incident.

"Just last night," Dad said. "Out in the country this time, on Blackberry Road. They got some sheep farmer's prizewinning herd dog. A Border collie, I think they said."

"They did? A herding dog? A collie?" David was so surprised that he couldn't think what to say, so he just kept repeating what Dad was saying. And when there wasn't anything more to repeat he just went on talking without thinking: "I guess that's why they didn't try for Mayor Sam last night."

"Mayor Sam?" Dad asked.

Realizing what he'd gotten himself into, David gulped. "Uh, yeah. We—uh, Garvey and Amanda and I —we had this theory that they might get Mayor Sam next. You know, that old bloodhound type that hangs around the mall?"

"Why did you think that?" Dad asked.

"Because most people in Steven's Corners are keeping their dogs shut up now, especially after dark. And Sam's always right there running loose, day and night."

"Umm. Possibility, I guess," Dad said, and turned the radio back up.

Amanda came in then, and soon afterward the rest of the kids. Dad and Molly didn't say any more about the new dog theft, and David didn't either. In fact, David didn't say much of anything during the meal. And nobody said anything to Dad and Molly about being arrested and taken to the police station.

David hadn't told anybody not to tell. He'd thought about it a lot on the way home last night, and afterward, when he was in bed. At first he thought he would; he'd just mention to everyone that it would be better not to say anything about what had happened. After all, it wasn't as if they'd really done something illegal and been booked and everything, because they hadn't. The only reason it might be better not to tell about it was just that if they did, they'd have to get into why they followed Sam to the park. And that meant telling that the kids hadn't gone to the Disney movie, and that would bring up the fact that Janie was still involved in trying to solve mysteries, not to mention the fact that David had sort of—well, almost—said she could go on helping with his stolen dog investigation.

But on the other hand, David didn't like the idea of telling the little kids to keep something from Dad and Molly. So the way it turned out he decided not to decide what to do. Instead he'd just wait it out and see what happened. And if the kids started talking about it he'd take it from there and tell Dad the whole story.

But they didn't. Nobody said a word about the park or Officer Wilmot or the police station. Instead Janie brought up the subject of the school fair and the kinds of booths each classroom was going to have. So the little kids rattled on about ring toss booths and fishing booths and dunk-the-principal booths and which classes were going to do which. Amanda didn't say anything much, except to complain because there wasn't any more nonfat milk, which was going to ruin her dieting program for the entire week.

Dad and Molly listened to the radio for a while longer, and then they turned it off and started talking about what the newscaster had said. They didn't ask anybody any questions.

At the time David was so busy wondering who was going to say what, and what Dad was going to say if they did, that it didn't even occur to him to think about the

Trans. In fact, he didn't start worrying about what the new dog theft would mean to them until the paper came. But when he read the story in the *Valley Press* he suddenly starting thinking about how this new dognapping story might affect Mr. Wright—and the Trans.

The story was just a short item on the third page. All it said was that another theft had taken place and that the latest missing dog was a highly trained herd dog that belonged to a sheep farmer named Ian McGarrity. According to the story the McGarritys were offering a reward for any information leading to the return of their dog.

Reading the article, David suddenly felt depressed. If Mr. Wright did decide to sell out, things looked bad for the Tran family, and there didn't seem to be anything David or anyone else could do about it. And then there was the investigative reporting project for Mr. Edmonds's class, which didn't seem to be in very good shape either.

David cut out the article and got out his news story folder. He spread out all the stuff from the folder on the dining room table: the newspaper clippings, the library research notes and the notes from the interviews, the photographs, and the project proposal with the big red "A" on it. There was a lot of material there, but none of it seemed to be going anywhere. It certainly didn't seem to be heading toward a solution to the mystery, or even to a logical ending for the final write-up. He'd been hoping to get started on the writing in a day or two, but now, with the new theft, it looked as if there would have to be a least one more interview. He sighed.

Then he went out to the hall phone and called Pete Garvey.

Mrs. Garvey answered the phone, and when David told her who was calling she said, "David? Oh, yes. I've been wondering about you and that newspaper story. Junior hasn't said a thing about your assignment lately. Won't talk about it at all, in fact. I've been wondering how it's going."

"Well," David said, "it's been going pretty well, I guess. But I think we're going to need to do at least one more investigative interview. That's what I wanted to talk to Pete about."

"Sure enough," Mrs. Garvey said. "I'll go get him. You just hold on a minute. I think he's out helping his dad change the oil in the truck."

While David waited he thought about the best approach to take with Garvey. He'd been acting so strange lately that David had begun to worry that he might be getting ready to drop out of the whole project. And that would mean starting all over with a new partner, or else finishing it up by himself, either of which would be a real drag. It would be best, he decided, not to mention Garvey's weird behavior and to act as if everything were just fine.

So when Pete picked up the phone David said, "Hi, Garvey. I just called to tell you that it looks like we're going to have to do another interview before we write up our story."

There was a long pause before Garvey said, "Oh yeah? Why's that?"

"Well, it looks like there has been another dog stolen. A sheepherding dog out on Blackberry Road."

On the other end of the line there was a loud clattering noise.

"What's the matter, Garvey? Garvey? You drop the phone or something?"

After a few seconds Garvey came back on the line. "Yeah," he said. "Yeah. I dropped the phone. My hand's greasy, I guess. Did you say on Blackberry Road?"

"It was in today's paper. Some kind of collie that belonged to a sheep farmer named McGarrity. I guess we'd better go out and talk to him before we start writing up the story. What do you think?"

Again there was a silence, and then a long string of muttering sounds, as if Garvey were talking to himself. David couldn't hear much of it, but he did make out a word here and there, words like *crazy* and *stupid* and a few four-letter words that Garvey used now and then when he was angry.

After that there was another silence, and then Pete said, "I dunno. About going out to McGarrity's. I been pretty busy, lately. I don't think I have time to go way out there. You shouldn't ought to go out there either."

David was puzzled. "Why not?"

"Well . . . uh, you just shouldn't ought to." There was a long pause, and then, "Them McGarritys are real unfriendly types. They're not going to tell you anything. Going out there's just going to be a waste of time. I've heard about them McGarritys for years, and what I hear is that they're real unfriendly. They'll probably just chase you off the place or something."

David was beginning to get the picture, and it was making him angry. He didn't get angry very often, and when he did it always gave him a pain in the stomach.

At that moment he was really mad, and the pain in his stomach made him even madder.

"Look," he said, "unfriendly doesn't bother me. They couldn't be much more unfriendly than Mrs. Ferris was at first, and we got a lot of good stuff from her. Besides, I don't think that's what the problem is. What the problem is is that you're finking out on me. You got me to say we'd be partners, and you got me to do most of the work, too, and then you fink out on me. All I can say is that you're some friend. With friends like you, Garvey, I'll take unfriendly any day."

David was breathing hard. On the other end of the line he could hear Garvey breathing hard too. David could just see him. He could just imagine Garvey's big flat face with the mean smile he always got when he was angry. The breathing went on and on, and then Garvey finally said something, but what he said didn't sound angry. David couldn't believe what it did sound like.

"Stanley," the strange shaky voice said. "I'm sorry. I'm sorry, Stanley." And then the phone went dead.

Chapter 15

After the weird phone conversation with Pete Garvey, David came back to the dining room and just sat there, thinking for a while, trying to figure out what in the ever loving blue-eyed world was going on. Considering how crazy Pete had been about the whole reporting project at first, the way he'd been acting lately was really off the wall. Of course, a lot of his interest in working with David could have been because it gave him a chance to see more of Amanda, but that didn't explain the big change. Amanda was still treating him about the same as she always had—which maybe wasn't the greatest, but in the past it hadn't seemed to discourage him much. There just wasn't any logical explanation for the whole thing.

He was still puzzling about it when Janie went past the dining room door. He called to her to come in.

"Look," he said, giving her the article about the stolen collie. "Did Dad or Molly tell you about this?"

Janie read the article, threw it down on the table, stared at David with big eyes, and ran out of the room. A few seconds later he heard her talking on the hall phone. He couldn't quite hear what she was saying, but from the tone of her voice he knew that the conversation wasn't making her feel any better. After a few minutes she came back into the room, and before she said anything he could tell that the news was really bad. Janie looked as if she were about to cry.

"The Trans?" David asked.

She nodded. "Mr. Wright fired them. He came over this morning and told Mr. Tran he had just till the end of the month to find a new job and somewhere to live. Thuy was crying." And Janie sat down at the table and put her head down and started to cry too. Actually Janie cried pretty often, but usually it was just a put-on. This time it wasn't.

David sighed. "Listen, Janie. Maybe we can do something. Maybe we can . . . Well, I'm going out to talk to these latest people whose dog was stolen. Maybe this time I'll find something out that will help clear the Trans. I'll bet I do; I have a feeling that this time I'm going to learn something that will really help."

He wasn't just making it up to make Janie feel better, either. He suddenly did have one of his premonitions. Like most premonitions it wasn't very clear. It wasn't so much that he knew he was going to find out who the dog thieves were; it was a little more general than that. What it felt like was that something was going to happen. Something important.

Janie raised her head. Her eyes and cheeks were wet and there were several little tear pools on the table. She had always cried the biggest, wettest tears in the world. If crying were an Olympic event Janie would be a gold medalist. Sniffing and gulping, she blinked her long eyelashes, which were stuck together in dark shiny clumps. Then she wiped her face with both hands and smiled a quivery smile. "I'll go too," she said.

David's first impulse was to say no. He knew that no was always the safest impulse where Janie was concerned. But he also thought he knew what would happen if he did. "What happens if I say no?" he asked.

Janie's face began to crumple and another wave of tears spilled down her cheeks. David sighed. "Yeah," he said. "I thought so."

He checked his watch. It was only one o'clock. "Okay. We'll go right now. I'll check with Dad, and if he says okay we'll go right away."

Janie was still rubbing tears off her face and swallowing leftover sobs. "Will Dad let us?" she asked.

"Well, I'm pretty sure he'll let me. I'll just tell him that I want to interview the McGarritys and—"

"And you can say that the twins and I want to go along too because it's a sheep ranch and I'm studying about sheep ranches at school."

"Get real," David said, grinning.

"We are. We really are. The third grade always studies about the county and all the farms and business and things like that. Don't you remember that from when you were in third grade? And we're all going to have to write a report about the way people earn their living in our county. And I'm going to write about sheep ranching. I've just decided."

"Wow!" David shook his head. Dad was right when he said that Janie would make a great lawyer someday. She could think up good arguments faster than anybody in the whole world. "It just might work," he said. "Come on. It's worth a try. But you'd better wash your face first."

"How about Amanda?" Janie asked as they were on their way up the stairs a few minutes later.

"She's not here," David said. Molly and Amanda had gone in to spend the day with some friends in the apartment building where they used to live before Molly and Dad got married.

"I know," Janie said. "But won't she be mad at us for going without her?"

"She might. But we've got to get going on this. There isn't much time."

Janie nodded hard. "Yes. We'll just have to go without her."

On second thought, David was kind of hoping that Dad would let the little kids go with him to the McGarrity sheep ranch. It wasn't just because he felt sorry for Janie. It was more that he couldn't help feeling a little nervous about going out there all alone after what Pete had said about the McGarritys being so unfriendly. Not that the little kids would be any protection or anything like that—at least, not against anything really dangerous. But against plain old unfriendliness they just might be. David had found by experience that having three little kids along, particularly three seriously cute types like Janie and the twins, was a real plus in some situations. In fact, Blair was practically an insurance policy against unfriendliness all by himself.

Dad was in the midst of writing a proposal about a field trip he wanted to take his students on, and it was pretty obvious he wasn't too thrilled about being interrupted. So after he'd given David permission to go and Janie had made her pitch about researching sheep ranches, David slipped in a little hint about how much more peace and quiet there'd be around the house if the kids went with him.

"We'll be gone for quite a while," he finished up. "We'll have to take the Andersen bus out to to where it turns back and then walk up Blackberry Road for about a mile. We probably won't be home till almost dinnertime."

"Hmm," Dad said with a wistful look on his face. "That's true. It would take most of the afternoon, I suppose. And the twins too? You want to take the twins too? I have to admit I could do without any more interruptions from them this afternoon. They've been in here three or four times since lunch. The last time it was to borrow my camera to take pictures of Nightmare."

"I don't mind taking them too," David said.

"Yes," Janie said. "That way they can get a head start on learning about sheep ranching for when they're in third grade."

David grinned. "That's what I call really starting your homework early."

"But they'll remember all about it," Janie said. "Visiting a sheep ranch is the kind of thing you remember all your life."

Dad threw up his hands in surrender. "All right, Janie. You win—but wait a minute. Come back here."

Janie had started out of the room. She came back and Dad put his hands on her shoulders. "I'm letting you go, but I want you to remember that I'm trusting you to do exactly what David says, and not make a nusiance of yourself in any way." Where Janie was concerned Dad never had been very realistic.

As David was leaving, Dad said that it might be a good idea to call the McGarritys first to see if it was a convenient time for them to be interviewed.

"Yeah," David said. "It might." Actually he'd already thought about it and decided against it. If the McGarritys were as unfriendly as Garvey said they were, they'd be sure to say no if you asked ahead of time. But they'd have to be world-class unfriendly to say no when you were standing on their doorstep, particularly if you had three cute little kids with you.

He found Blair and Esther in the side yard playing with Nightmare. Esther had put Dad's old rain slicker and a sun hat of Molly's on him, and she was trying to get him to hold an old pipe of Dad's in his mouth while she took his picture. Nightmare was being patient about the slicker and hat, but every time she put the pipe in his mouth he spit it out.

"Nightmare's being bad," Esther said. "He'll hold a stick or a ball in his mouth if I tell him to, but he won't hold Dad's pipe. And Blair won't tell him he has to. He'd do it if Blair told him he had to."

"It's because it smells smoky," Blair said. "Dogs are too smart to put smoky stuff in their mouths."

When the the twins heard about the trip to the sheep

ranch they ran off to get ready, and Janie went with them to hurry them up. David stayed behind to get the raincoat off Nightmare. It took quite a bit of tugging and pulling, and when it was finally off, Nightmare licked David's face three or four times and bounced around him all the way back into the house, wagging his tail.

By the time David had found his notebook and tape recorder the little kids were ready to go, and they made it out to the road in time to catch the one thirty bus into Steven's Corners. After arriving in town they had to walk three or four blocks to a different bus stop and wait for the one that went out Andersen Road. Then they rode about five or six miles out into the country to where the route ended. After that they started walking.

It wasn't a bad walk. The road sloped gently upward, and on each side were apple orchards and open fields. The apple trees were still bare, but the fields were green from the recent rains, and here and there were big yellow patches where wild mustard was starting to bloom. The sun was low, but there was still some warmth in it, and the air had the cool green taste of growing things. David would have enjoyed it if he hadn't had Garvey's warning about the McGarritys sliding around in the back of his head.

One thing he didn't have to worry about was getting lost. Blackberry Road was familiar to the whole Stanley family because it was a shortcut to Sunset Park, which was one of Molly's favorite picnic and painting places. The way David remembered it, the McGarrity ranch was in the foothills just a little way past the old Springer place. They'd been walking about fifteen minutes when to the right of the road the old farm buildings came into view.

The Springer farm had been a dairy until recently. There was an old box-shaped two-story house near the road, and behind it a lot of other buildings, a milking barn and one for hay and a bunch of smaller sheds. In the past the surrounding fields had always been full of black and white cows, but now the cows were gone. It wasn't until they got to the lane leading down to the farmhouse that David remembered something: according to Garvey, Ace Maillard's friends, the car-crazy Potters, were now living on the Springer place.

"Keep your eyes open," he told the little kids. "This is where those screwball hot-rod drivers live. If a car comes along, get off the road. Way off."

"You mean those guys who almost ran over Blair?" Janie asked.

"Yeah. At least I think so. Or else it was Mack Maillard. I couldn't tell for sure."

The little kids got way off the road and walked along in the weeds, staring at every car that went by. But nothing came in or out of the Springer driveway, and there was no sound except the deep, harsh barking of a dog.

The road was steeper now, and as they got farther up the slope they could look down across the Springer property and see that there were cars and parts of cars all around the yard, scattered between the outbuildings and clear down to where a big grove of trees lined the banks of a stream. In front of the farmhouse a large black dog was chained to a tree. The dog was on his feet, looking toward the Stanleys and barking steadily.

The kids stopped to look and David came back to join them.

"I liked the cows better," Janie said.

"Me too," David said. "It looks like a junkyard now."

Esther climbed up on the fence to see better. "Look at that poor dog," she said. "He's chained up. Poor dog."

Blair climbed up beside her. "Poor dog," he said. "Poor doggies."

A little farther up the hill they came to the entrance of the McGarrity sheep ranch. A curving gravel road led back to a big old ranch house in the shade of some enormous oak trees.

David was having second thoughts as they started down the long drive. He was thinking about Garvey's warning and wondering just how unfriendly the Mc-Garritys were going to be, when a man came out from behind the house. He was one of the biggest men David had ever seen, and his huge round head covered with lots of grayish-blond hair made him look like a scruffy old lion. The minute he spotted David and the kids he changed directions and came striding toward them.

David stopped in his tracks, and for just a moment he considered yelling "Run!" The big man came on down the driveway, roaring something in a loud deep voice. It wasn't until he'd yelled it a second time that David figured out that he was saying, "Well, hello there, strangers. Welcome to the McGarrity ranch."

As David found himself being escorted up the driveway along with Janie and the twins, it did occur to him that his cute-kid unfriendliness insurance had worked surprisingly fast. But then, he forgot all about Garvey's warning.

"Ma," Mr. McGarrity called as he led the way across a wide veranda and into an old-fashioned parlor. "Ma, come on out here. We have company."

Mrs. McGarrity looked like she was made up to play a role in a television commercial, one of those commercials about frozen pies that taste just like the ones Grandma used to make. The scene is this old-fashioned kitchen with checkered tablecloths and ruffled windows and then Grandma comes on the screen carrying a pie. She's wearing a grandmotherly-type dress with an apron over it, and there's this big smile spread all across her face. When Mrs. McGarrity first came into the room David found himself looking for the pie. Actually it turned out to be cookies instead of pie, and it came a little later, but the rest of it was right out of the commercial.

But before that, both the McGarritys made a big fuss over the little kids, asking their names and ages and what grades they were in at school. And Mrs. McGarrity kept carrying on about how much Esther looked like one of their grandchildren, who lived someplace a long way off.

It took quite a long time before they got around to David, but when they did and he told them about his news story assignment they were almost as enthusiastic about that. David explained about how he had interviewed the other people who'd lost dogs and how he was hoping that he might find out something that would help to catch the thieves. To his surprise Mr. McGarrity actually seemed to think that he might.

"Good thinking, young man," he said in his booming voice. "Good thinking. You make enough comparisons and something just might sift out that would help the police. It would sure mean a lot to Louella and me if you did come up with something. We're just real certain that the same bunch that took all the others was responsible for our Lad's disappearance as well. We've offered a five-hundred-dollar reward, and we'd be only to glad to pay it if someone could just find our Lad for us."

Mr. McGarrity went on and on about their missing dog. He was a Border collie whose full name was Highland Lad of Blue Mountain, and he'd won all sorts of prizes at sheepherding competitions. The McGarritys brought out some of his ribbons and trophies, and scrapbooks full of pictures and newspaper articles. David turned on his tape recorder and got it all taped, including all the dope about where Lad usually slept and what had happened the night he disappeared.

After David had asked all the questions he could think of, Mrs. McGarrity insisted that they go out to the kitchen and have cookies and hot chocolate. It wasn't until they were sitting around the big old round kitchen table that David got around to remembering Garvey's warning.

He was sitting there happily drinking his cocoa when suddenly he found himself thinking "real unfriendly types." Real unfriendly types, he thought to himself, and didn't know whether to laugh or what. The "or what" was, what if Garvey was really crazy? Or what if somebody else was?

The thing was that there just wasn't any way you could call the McGarritys' behavior unfriendly, not unless it was all an act. A phony-friendly act like maybe the friendly spider's invitation to the fly, or the witch's friendly invitation to Hansel and Gretel.

David froze for a minute, staring into his hot chocolate. When he looked up it was just in time to see Mrs. McGarrity coming out of the pantry with more cookies, smiling her wraparound smile. His answering smile felt pasted on.

Chapter 16

David's sudden panic attack about the McGarritys didn't last very long. Watching Ian and Louella—the McGarritys insisted on being called Ian and Louella—chatting up the little kids and urging everyone to have more cookies, it just wasn't easy to go on suspecting them of being smiling-spider types, or welcoming witches either. They just didn't look or act the part. Either they were the real thing or they were a pair of world-class actors.

That thought, however, did trigger a sudden return to the panic button. In the movies and on TV there were always these crazy killers and other antisocial types who could put on super-nice-guy faces until somebody laughed at them or the moon was full or something like that. And then look out. David checked out Ian McGarrity again—and had to grin.

Blair was sitting on Ian's lap and talking to him about

Nightmare; talking a lot, for Blair. And that in itself was pretty good proof that Ian was what he seemed to be—a real nice guy. Because if he wasn't, Blair would know it. Blair might not always know the difference between pretending and reality, as Dad said, but he'd always been good at knowing the difference between a pretend friend and a real one. And it was pretty plain that Blair thought that Ian McGarrity was the real thing.

So David calmed down and went on with his chocolate and cookies, and when everyone finished, Ian took them all out to the farmyard to see the the sheep ranch operation. First they went through the barn and the lambing pens.

In the barn they met Ian's only remaining herd dog, a female named Sarah's Sunrise, and her litter of puppies, and there were two early lambs in the lambing pens. It was all interesting, and of course the little kids went batty over the lambs and puppies.

Next they went on around the yard looking at things like shearing sheds and the dipping tank. Janie was asking questions and writing stuff in her notebook and being the center of attention as usual, when David suddenly noticed that Blair was missing.

"Hey," he said. "Where's Blair?"

Nobody seemed to know, but Esther thought he might have gone back to see the puppies again. So they looked for him in the barn, but he wasn't there, and he wasn't at the lambs' pen either. David began to get worried. He went across the barnyard so as not to scare the mother sheep and began to shout at the top of his lungs.

He'd been yelling, "Blair! Blair! Where are you,

Blair?" for quite a while before he heard an answering shout and saw Blair running up the hill that sloped down from the McGarrity property toward the old Springer farm.

"Here I come. Here I come, David," Blair was calling.

He didn't say exactly where he'd been or why he'd gone off by himself. When David asked him he only rolled his eyes and said, "Down there," and when David asked him what he'd been doing he frowned and nodded for a while before he said, "Looking. I was just looking—and thinking."

It was obvious that he wasn't going to say any more, and it was getting late, so David blasted him a little about wandering off and worrying everybody and then let the whole thing drop. They went back to the barn, where Ian was still looking for Blair in the hayloft and Janie and Esther had gotten sidetracked by the puppies and forgotten all about searching for their missing brother.

When Ian climbed down from the loft David told him they were going to have to leave. Ian called to Louella to come out of the house, and after a lot of good-byes and thank-yous and even hugs and kisses for the little kids, they were finally on their way.

On the Andersen Road bus David did some more thinking—and worrying. Janie was writing in her notebook and Blair and Esther were half asleep, so David had quite a bit of free time in which to drive himself crazy.

What he worried about first was Pete Garvey. He was beginning to feel really nervous about poor old Pete. At first, when Pete started being so silent and distant, he'd thought that he was angry about something, or just in a bad mood, but it was beginning to look more serious than that. A bad mood might explain why he backed out of the newspaper article project. And it might possibly explain why he wouldn't go on the Mayor Sam caper, even though Amanda was going to be there. But there was just no logical explanation for what he'd said about the McGarritys being so unfriendly. And then there was his strange un-Garvey-like reaction when David got angry at him. The only explanation seemed to be that Pete Garvey was cracking up.

It took a while for David to convince himself that since there wasn't anything he could do about Garvey's problems there was no point in worrying about them. But that left a few other things to start in on, like the stolen dogs, and the Tran family's problem, and whether Mr. Edmonds would let him finish the article without a partner.

After several minutes of high-level, brain-rotting-type anxiety he finally pulled himself together and decided to try something more productive, such as going over the information he'd gotten from the McGarritys about the disappearance of Highland Lad.

Lad, Mr. McGarrity said, usually spent the evenings in the farmhouse until the McGarritys went to bed. Then they put him outside. For the rest of the night he slept in the barn, but the small side door was left open so he could go out into the barnyard. That was so he could keep skunks and raccoons away from the chicken run and garbage pails. Lad wasn't much of a barker except when critters came around, Mr. McGarrity said, and he almost never barked at human beings.

On the night that he was stolen Lad was put outside around ten o'clock, and the McGarritys never heard him bark or any other kind of disturbance during the night. And since the barnyard was fenced there wasn't any way he could have just wandered off or run away.

Except for the fact that Lad had disappeared later in the evening, this case was similar to the others, and just as lacking in important clues. David went over and over all the details in his mind, comparing them to what he'd learned from the other dog owners. But nothing came together in a way that told him anything special about the thieves, like who they were or what their motive might be for stealing other people's dogs.

After they'd changed buses and the twins had completely flaked out, Janie leaned over Esther and asked in a whisper if he knew who the dognappers were yet. David said no, but that he was still working on it. She said okay, that she'd be quiet and let him think. "But be sure to tell me the minute you get it figured out," she said, and he promised that he would. The way she said it made him worry more than ever, like she was certain that his so-called premonition was right and that this time he was really going to come up with something that would crack the whole dognapping case wide open.

David was still thinking in brain-numbing circles when the bus started up the last slope before the old Westerly house and it was time to start getting the twins awake enough to get off the bus.

At dinner that night the little kids talked a lot about

the sheep ranch, and Amanda had quite a few things to say about her visit with her old friend, Leah, whom she hadn't seen for a long time. Leah, according to Amanda, had turned into a real spaz. Amanda had a lot to say about all the things she and Leah disagreed on and the interests they didn't have in common any longer. So quite a bit of the dinnertime conversation was either about Leah or the McGarritys. There wasn't much opportunity for David to say anything at all, which was a good thing, because he really didn't feel like it.

He was still feeling the same way later that night when Janie came into his room to talk. He had just gotten into bed, and across the room Blair was already sound asleep. Nightmare and all the rest of Blair's menagerie were asleep too, Nightmare on his mattress, Rolor on his perch, and the mouse and snake and hamster in their cages. A couple of minutes later and David might also have been asleep too, or at least have had the lights out so that he could have pretended to be. But Janie beat him to it.

She came in on tiptoe, climbed up on the foot of his bed, and sat herself down cross-legged. She was wearing her pajamas and her face was still slick and shiny from her bath, and little wet corkscrew curls were hanging down the back of her neck.

"Well?" she said, smiling eagerly as if she were expecting to hear some really exciting news.

"Well what?" David said.

"Well, what happened? What important thing happened today, like you said was going to? Like you said you had a premonition about?" Janie had always been big on premonitions.

David sighed inwardly. It was late, and he was tired, and he wasn't in the mood for coping with any more weeping and wailing. "Well," he said, "some good stuff happened. Like meeting the McGarritys and seeing the puppies and lambs and—"

"I don't mean that." Janie was frowning. "I mean *important* things. Things that'll help us find out who the dognappers are."

David thought fast. "Well, I don't know for sure yet. But I'm pretty sure it happened. The important thing, I mean." He stopped to think. "You know how in detective books and TV shows somebody's always having this feeling that the answer is right there in front of him, but he just hasn't quite seen it yet?"

"Yes." Janie nodded hard.

"Well that's how I feel right now. The important thing happened today, but we haven't quite realized it yet. I'm still working on it."

Janie didn't look convinced, but at least she didn't start bawling again. After she'd gone back to her room David turned off the light and started trying to go to sleep. But the funny thing was that he found he'd started believing what he'd told Janie. He'd started feeling sure something very *important* had happened today, and that pretty soon he was going to find out what it had been, if he kept working on it.

He was still working on it when the hall clock struck eleven, and he was still working on it sometime after that when he finally went to sleep—or more like, passed out from sheer brain exhaustion. The next morning he was still working on it.

The whole next week was kind of a drag. The days stretched out until each one seemed a week long, and the nights were even worse. In the evenings, along with his other homework, David was trying to get going on the final write-up of the Steven's Corners disappearing dogs story, without much success. The problem was that the story was supposed to be finished and turned in at the end of the next week, and there just didn't seem to be any good way to finish a story about an event that hadn't ended. Dogs were still disappearing, and no one knew who the thieves were. It seemed to David that writing a human interest article about an unfinished current event was a lot like writing a detective story about an unsolved mystery, and the results were going to be just about as satisfying.

And then there was the problem of what to tell Mr. Edmonds about who had and who hadn't worked on the story. According to Edmonds's instructions, the finished report was to be accompanied with an outline of the work that each of the partners had done and how many hours they'd each put in on the assignment. David hadn't started work on the outline, and he hadn't yet told Mr. Edmonds that Garvey had quit. Not that there was any real doubt about it. Garvey had finked out on him, and he was going to get an "F" on the assignment, and that was all there was to it. But still, David wanted one more chance to talk to him. He'd ask him once more what his plans were, and then if nothing seemed to be changing he'd tell Mr. Edmonds that the Stanley-Garvey partnership was over. Finished. Kaput!

But Garvey was obviously avoiding him. All week long David kept trying to talk to him, before class or afterward, and all week long Garvey managed to show up late and leave early, or to start talking to a lot of other people so David couldn't say anything to him that he didn't want the whole school to know about.

One evening he even tried to phone him again.

Mrs. Garvey answered, and when she found out who it was she said she'd get Junior, but she didn't. When she came back to the phone she said, "He says he can't come to the phone right now, David." Her voice was slow, with a puzzled and worried sound to it.

"Oh," David said. "Well, I guess I'll catch him later."

There was a long pause, and then Mrs. Garvey said, "You boys have a little scrap, or somethin'?"

"A scrap?" David asked.

"A fight."

David smiled, thinking that there was no way to have a "little" fight with Pete Garvey. Having a little fight with Pete Garvey was like being a little bit dead. "No," he said. "No fight. I guess he's just been pretty busy lately. I'll catch him later at school, Mrs. Garvey. Thanks a lot."

Finally, on Friday morning, David arrived early and hung out near Garvey's locker until he showed up. Standing behind a trophy case he waited until Pete was dialing his combination and then sneaked toward him on the other side of the hall. "Hey, Garvey," he said when he was only a few feet away, "I've got to talk to you."

Garvey whirled around with an expression on his face a lot like Esther's when she got caught with her head in the refrigerator scarfing stuff Molly had put off limits. What he looked like was G-U-I-L-T, with a capital everything. "Uh . . . oh, hi, Stanley." Pete glanced around nervously as if he were looking for someone to come to his rescue. "Where'd you come from?"

"Where'd I come from?" David hunched his shoulders and did a robot number. "I come from outer space," he said in a mechanical-type voice. "I was sent to this planet to disintegrate fink-outs." Then he got serious. "Seriously, Garvey, I have to know what your plans are about the article. Are you out for good, or what?"

Garvey hung his head. Then he shuffled around, twisting his shoulders and rocking back and forth as if he were in some kind of awful pain. When he finally raised his head the expression on his face was so miserable that for a minute David flashed on a sudden-death theory, like maybe Garvey had some kind of fatal disease and he'd nobly backed out of the assignment because he knew he wasn't going to live to finish it.

"Pete?" he said. "You sick or something?"

"Naw." Garvey shook his head. "I'm okay. I just can't work on that dog story no more. And don't ask me why." Suddenly his expression was more familiar— threatening. He reached out and grabbed David's shoulder and squeezed it—hard. "You hear me? Don't ask me about it no more!"

David got the message. From now on the newspaper story was all up to him. Garvey would get an "F" for sure, but that was his problem. David's problem, along with a few others, was that Mr. Edmonds had said that the assignment was partly to see how well you could work as a team. Part of your grade, Mr. Edmonds said, would depend on evidence of good teamwork. So David's grade was pretty much at risk too.

The day got off to a pretty rotten start, and it didn't get much better as it went along. In Ms. Baldwin's class David tripped over someone's feet and fell across Holly Rayburn's desk and knocked all her books onto the floor. Lunch in the cafeteria featured a nauseating brussels sprout quiche, and in gym class his volleyball serve, which was usually pretty good, was rock bottom awful.

David was still in a bad mood that evening when he got home and slammed through the back door into the kitchen. He banged his books down on the table and started rummaging around for an after-school snack. Of course the cookie jar was empty. Of course it was. Cookies and milk would be too easy. He was still slamming things around making himself a peanut butter sandwich when Molly came out of the pantry carrying a magazine and her new recipe file.

"Oh, it's you," she said, looking surprised.

"Yeah," David said. "Me. Who'd you think it was?"

"Oh, I don't know. I thought it might be Amanda."

David almost grinned, thinking that he had made an Amanda-type entrance, all right. Amanda in a bad mood was a world-class slammer and stomper. "Yeah," he said. "I can see why." And then he started telling Molly about his rotten day. He didn't go into the Garvey problem, but he told her about landing in Holly's lap and the sickening quiche and the even more sickening volleyball game. And by the time he got through he was feeling a little better.

Molly was cutting some recipes out of the magazine

and adding them to her file. Ever since New Year's she'd been into collecting recipes. David didn't know if it was some kind of a New Year's resolution or just Mrs. Dorfman's famous broadcast about her cooking. But either way it hadn't made much of a difference, as far as David could see. Molly still burned stuff a lot, only lately she'd been burning soufflés and casseroles instead of lamb chops and hamburgers. But when David started in about his lousy day she put down her scissors and listened. When he'd finally finished his tale of woe she sighed and nodded and asked him if he'd like some more milk.

"Yeah," David said in a sloppy-drunk-type voice. "Fill 'er up, bartender. Might as well drown my sorrows."

Molly filled his glass and patted him on the shoulder and said to cheer up because the good news was that tomorrow was bound to be better. "For one thing, it's Saturday," she said. "Saturdays are always better. Right?"

"Right," David said loudly, trying to drown out a sneaky inner voice that seemed to be saying, *Wrong!*

Chapter 17

Saturday morning was pretty routine. After she'd more or less done her weekend chores, Amanda went off on the bus to visit her friend Tammy. David might have gone somewhere, too, except that Molly and Jeff had a reception to go to, and David was the designated baby-sitter for the afternoon. He didn't mind too much. The Tran kids were coming over, and so there wouldn't be any question of having to entertain anybody. When Janie and the twins had company they usually entertained themselves. David was planning to read and relax and just check on the kids now and then to be sure they hadn't decided to invent a disintegrater or something. You never knew with Janie and Thuy. If those two put their heads together they just might be able to do it.

The Tran kids had been coming over to play quite often lately, but this time they were going to stay all weekend. Molly told David about it just before she and Dad left.

"The Trans are going to San Jose," she said. "They're taking the babies with them, but they have to go on the bus and they really can't afford seats for Thuy and Huy. Tien has a job possibility at a nursery near San Jose and he has to go check it out."

"Tien?" David asked.

"Mr. Tran," Molly said. Molly had gotten to be an authority on the Tran family lately. Ever since she found out that Mr. Tran had been fired she'd been talking to people she knew in town, trying to get them to sign a petition asking Mr. Wright to change his mind about selling the nursery. She'd also spent quite a lot of time at the nursery, and gotten to know the Trans really well. Molly said the Trans were beautiful people.

"I'm sorry we have to be away this afternoon," she told David. "But we promised the Bradleys months ago. And we won't be gone late. We'll be home in time for dinner. If you could just keep an eye on the kids until we get back."

David shrugged. "It's all right with me," he said. "They won't bother me. They'll probably just remodel the living room and bake mud pies in the microwave. I'll try not to get in their way."

Molly grinned at him and he said, "You think I'm kidding, don't you?"

"What I think is, you'd better be," Molly said.

The kids didn't remodel the living room, or invent a disintegrater either, but Thuy and Huy hadn't been there long when Janie did come up with an idea that upset David's read-and-relax plan. Janie decided that everybody wanted to go hiking. And of course that meant David had to go along.

Actually, David had always liked hiking in the hills behind the Westerly House. He'd really missed it when the escaped convict scare was on and the hills were off limits. One of the neat things about being at least partly responsible for the big capture was that the hills were no longer forbidden territory. He liked best to go alone, but he'd taken the little kids with him several times, and they hadn't been too much of a nuisance. But that had been three kids, and this time there would be five.

"I don't know," David said, frowning. "You'll all stay together and do what I tell you?"

They all nodded and went on nodding, like a bunch of perpetual-motion machines. All five of them had come into the living room a minute before and lined themselves up in front of the couch where he'd been reading a *National Geographic.* Because Janie and Thuy were so small for eight-year-olds they were all pretty much the same size, which was strictly minimodel humanity, except for Huy, who was more like supermini.

David put down his magazine and sat up. "You think Huy's big enough to climb up the steep places?"

Huy frowned fiercely. Then he marched forward until he was almost standing on David's feet. For just a minute David wondered if his ankles were safe, but he needn't have worried. Huy wasn't thinking of biting. Instead he pulled himself up to his full two feet, or whatever, and said, "Huy big enough. Huy climb *everything.* Okay?"

"Hey," David said to Thuy. "He's *speaking* English."

Thuy smiled and nodded. "I've been teaching him."

But Huy went on frowning. "Huy speaking everything," he said. "Okay?"

"Ooh-*kay*!" David said. "*So*— everybody go get your coats on."

"They're already on," Janie said.

David hadn't noticed before. "Right!" he said. "I guess you were pretty sure I'd say yes."

"Right," Janie said, grinning.

So David went to get his jacket, and in only a minute or two they were all on their way out the back door.

They weren't even down the porch steps when Nightmare came around the corner with his ears on alert. All dogs, Dad said, knew instinctively when anyone was even thinking about taking a walk, and Nightmare's instincts, like his size, were definitely top-of-the-line.

"David," Blair began. "Can Nightmare go—"

"Shh!" David interrupted. "Wait a minute, Blair." He finished locking the back door and then he grabbed Huy and held him up high. "Okay, take cover, everybody. Every man for himself." And then he said, "Okay, Nightmare. Want to go for a walk?" And one hundred sixty-five pounds of joy-crazed wolfhound went on a rampage.

While Nightmare celebrated by tearing around in circles, scattering the rest of the kids in all directions, David held Huy up out of harm's way. All five of the little kids were screaming with excitement, including Huy, who was screaming in David's ear. Right at that point David might have wondered what he'd gotten himself into, if he'd been able to hear himself think. But he wasn't, and he didn't, and after a minute or two everybody calmed down and the hike got under way.

It turned out that except for making David feel like a modern-day Pied Piper the hike itself was no problem. The little kids stayed together, and except for Tesser, who needed a few boosts, they went up the steep places like a swarm of monkeys. And when he asked them to be quiet so they could look for wild animals and birds they all quieted down in a hurry.

Nightmare was no problem either, since he was gone most of the time. On hikes in the hills he only checked in once in a while, in between hunting expeditions after mostly imaginary game, like maybe the ghosts of wolves his ancestors had hunted in olden times.

They got to the first ridge without any problems. If David hadn't insisted that they sit down and rest, the kids would have gone right on. But he did insist, so everyone rested for a few minutes, even Nightmare, who'd just caught up again after his latest tour through the underbrush.

Janie had been begging to go to the lake so she could show Thuy where David and Blair and Nightmare had captured the escaped convicts, and David had said okay. So after their rest stop they crossed the plateau and the second crest, and were starting down the last slope before the lake when David heard something that made him change his mind. The dirt bikers were out again.

"Okay, kids," he said. "I think this is as far as we go today."

"Why?" Janie said. "Why can't we go on?"

David explained about the dirt bikers. On weekends

a bunch of guys drove out Fillmore Road to the lake area to ride their dirt bikes in the hills, and when they did it messed up everything. Not only did the bikes tear up the hills and cause erosion and scare away the wild-life, but they were also dangerous.

"Most of them are crummy types like the Maillards," he said. "You know, those guys who probably were the ones who almost ran over Blair."

"Would they run over us if we went down there?" Blair asked.

"Who knows," David said. "They might." And he meant it too. It had occurred to him that he didn't want Ace Maillard or any of his buddies to see him playing nursemaid to a whole kindergarten, but that wasn't all of it. One of the kids might really get hit by some idiot on a dirt bike, the way they shot around the curves and up over the tops of hills. "I think maybe we'd better start back," he said. And although the little kids weren't happy about it, they didn't argue very much. They were halfway back up the second ridge before Blair began to fuss about finding Nightmare.

David couldn't remember seeing Nightmare since they'd stopped to rest, but he hadn't been gone much longer than usual. A couple of times on previous hikes David had given up on finding him and gone on home, and he'd turned up back at the house in an hour or two.

"He'll show up before long," David kept telling Blair. "He always does." But Blair went right on fussing about it.

They were almost home when he tugged on David's shirt. His eyes looked sad and a little bit teary. "David, I don't think Nightmare's just chasing something. I think he needs us."

David knew, of course, what Blair was thinking. He was remembering the time, before Nightmare was really their dog, when he'd cut his paw and hid out in a cave on the hill above the lake. "Look," he told Blair. "There isn't any reason to think anything like that has happened again. Now that he knows he's our dog, he'd just come on home if he got sick or hurt."

Blair nodded, but his oversize eyes were still doing a tragedy number. It wasn't until David promised to go back and look for Nightmare if he wasn't home in an hour or two that Blair seemed to cheer up a little.

Right after they got home the little kids started playing what looked like a fairly nondestructive game on the front veranda, so David went back to the living room couch. He stretched out with his magazine and promptly went to sleep. When he woke up a little while later, it was with a strong feeling that something was wrong.

For one thing, it was too quiet. He jumped up and went out to the front porch. No one was there, and it only took him a minute or two more to find out that there wasn't anyone anywhere in the house, or in the yard either. David stood in the middle of the back yard for a minute or two, calling as loud as he could, even though he knew by then that it was useless. The kids had definitely skipped out, and he was pretty sure he knew why, and where they'd gone. Blair had talked them into going back to look for Nightmare.

He dashed back to lock up the house and was on his way out again when he found the note. It was pinned to the front of his jacket and it was in Janie's handwriting. All it said was, *I have deduced where Nightmare is and we have gone to get him. We will be right back. Sincerely, Janie.* A few seconds later David was on his way back into the hills.

He went fast, jogging in the flatter places and scrambling up the steeper slopes. All the way he kept checking the path ahead of him, thinking he was sure to catch up with the kids soon. They couldn't have had very much of a head start, and he was covering the ground much faster than they possibly could. Once or twice he even stopped briefly to call. But there was no answer, and the path ahead of him went on being deserted.

He was pretty well winded when he reached the resting spot on the first ridge, but he pushed on across the mesa and up to the second crest. On the last slope before the lake he slid straight down the steep shortcuts on the zigzagging trail until he reached the path that led through the ravine and up to Nightmare's old cave. When he knew he was close enough to the cave to be heard, he stopped and shouted. He called Janie and Blair and even Nightmare, until he'd about used up all the breath he had left, but there was no answer. He was still standing there, wondering what to do next, when he heard the roar of a dirt bike, and immediately started toward the sound. If the kids had made it all the way to the lake, the bikers would probably have seen them.

The bike motor roared, sputtered, died, and then roared again, but it seemed to come always from one area, as if it was staying pretty much in the same spot. David followed the sound easily. He had crossed several bike trails, deep muddy scars on the green hillside, when the motor died again, and this time stayed dead. He kept on in the same general direction until he reached a thick clump of saplings and stopped, listening. Not far away someone was talking.

Pushing his way between the young trees, David suddenly came on a bunch of dirt bikes and one bike rider. The beat-up, muddy bikes had been shoved in among the saplings, and the rider was sitting on one of them, tromping on the starter and muttering to himself. The biker was Pete Garvey.

"Garvey?" David said, and Pete whirled around so fast that the bike tipped and he almost fell over getting off it.

"Stanley. Where'd you come from?" he said when he'd finally gotten back on his feet.

"From outer space," David said. "Look, Garvey, do we have to go through that again? Listen. Have you seen Janie, and the twins and some other little kids? I mean, have you seen any little kids around here?"

Garvey shook his head. "Naw. I haven't seen anybody. But I just got here. Ace and the other guys stopped by for me this morning, but my dad wouldn't let me go till I finished the sheds, so I just got here a few minutes ago, on my bike." He pointed to where his rickety old bicycle was leaning against one of the dirt bikes. "I dunno where the guys are, either. They never go off and leave their bikes. What makes you think the kids are around here?"

David started telling Pete how he and the kids and Nightmare had hiked almost to the lake and then turned back when they heard the bikers, and how

Nightmare had disappeared, and why he thought the kids had come back looking for him.

Garvey was listening hard, his eyes wide open. He kept coming closer and closer until he and David were almost nose to nose. When David finally stopped talking Pete stood there, looking as if someone had just hit him hard on the head and he was getting ready to pass out. At last he caught his breath and whirled around and started pounding his fist against one of the saplings. It wasn't much of a tree, and it was about to bend completely over when Garvey quit hitting it and started kicking the dirt bikes instead.

He went on kicking the bikes until they'd all tipped over, except one that was wedged in between two trees, and when it wouldn't fall down he grabbed it and yanked it out and threw it down the hill.

There was no doubt about it now: Garvey had completely cracked up. David was backing away, hoping he could get clear of the saplings and make a run for it, when Garvey quit attacking the bikes and sat down on the ground with his head on his knees. David stopped backing up and edged a little closer.

After a long time Pete raised his head a little and said, "Stanley?" and David said, "Yeah. I'm right here."

"Stanley," Pete said. "The guys did it. Mack and Ace and them Potters. They're the ones been stealing all the dogs. Some guy in the city is giving them lots of loot for all the classy dogs they can come up with. They probably got Nightmare. I was wondering why they'd go off and leave their bikes like this here. But I got it now. There wouldn't be room in the pickup for Nightmare and the bikes too." Garvey's voice faded out and he put his head back down on his knees.

David felt like his brain had just gone into overdrive and his legs had turned to spaghetti. He reached out and grabbed hold of the nearest sapling and stood there waiting for his thoughts to stop racing in circles and start making some sense. "Wha . . . wha . . . what?" he finally managed. "How do you know?"

"I know." Garvey's head was still down and his voice was muffled. He sat there a while longer before he lifted it up. "I've known for a long time. Ace told me because he wanted me to help them out, but I wouldn't." He turned to look at David. "Sure, Ace and me used to snitch little junk when we were kids, but I wouldn't take important stuff, like poor old lady Ferris's poodle. And then when you said they'd snatched McGarrity's sheepdog I was really pissed off."

"Why? Why did that make you madder than the others?"

"Because the McGarritys are real great people. I mean, they're nice to everybody, even the Potters, and then those creeps go and steal their dog. And besides, it was just a dumb thing to do. I mean, stealing your next-door neighbor's dog is not a very smooth move. Looks to me like they're just asking to get caught."

David was giving Pete an accusing stare, and he got the message. "Yeah, I know what I told you about the McGarritys, but that was a lie. I just told you because I was afraid if you went out there you might run into something dangerous, with the Potters being right next door and all."

"Yeah, but I still can't see how those guys could have

grabbed Nightmare. I mean, he's a lot more friendly to strangers now than he used to be, but if he didn't want to get into somebody's pickup it would take a lot more than four guys to put him in."

Pete nodded sadly. "They could have done it. They got this tranquilizer stuff this guy in the city gave them. Makes dogs go kind of limp and wimpy for a while. They could have used some of that on Nightmare."

David was beginning to feel angry. "Why'd you go along with all this, Garvey? I mean, why didn't you . . . ?"

Garvey's head dropped again and it was a minute or two before he raised it and said, "You mean, why didn't I rat on them? Yeah. Well, I wanted to. But Ace and me go back a long ways—clear to kindergarten. And besides, not ratting is just about the number-one rule. You know what I mean?"

David sighed and nodded. "Yeah, I guess so, only sometimes—"

"Hey!" All of a sudden Garvey jumped up, grabbed David's jacket, and yanked him up onto his toes. "What'd that note say, again? That note Janie pinned on your coat?"

"It said that she'd deduced where Nightmare was and—"

"Yeah," Garvey interrupted. "I'll bet she did, too. That kid can deduce like nobody's business." He jumped to his feet and charged down the hill to where he'd thrown the biggest bike. "Come on," he yelled at David. "We'll use Mack's. It's the fastest."

David slid down the hill after him. Garvey was tromping on the starter and the bike roared to life just as David climbed on the back. "Where are we going?" he yelled.

"To find Janie," Garvey yelled back. "To find Janie before she gets herself in a lot of big trouble."

Chapter 18

For the first couple of miles David just hung on to Garvey's leather jacket and tried not to listen to a conversation that seemed to be going on in the back of his brain. The thing was that now that he had committed himself by climbing on the back of the dirt bike, some inner voice seemed to be telling him that he'd made a mistake. The voice had quite a bit to say as Garvey steered the lurching bike through a ditch and across a hay field and out onto a dirt road. Like most of David's inner voices, it was fairly sarcastic. *Face it, Stanley,* it said, *this particular Saturday afternoon just possibly might not turn out to be your finest hour.*

Among other things, the voice pointed out that it was getting late, and pretty soon Dad and Molly would be coming home to find an empty house and not so much as an explaining note on the bulletin board. And in the meantime here he, David Stanley, was, roaring down back roads that he'd never seen before on the back of Mack Maillard's dirt bike, driven by Pete Garvey, who, as far as David knew, didn't have a license to drive anything. And as to why he'd gotten into such as mess, he could think of a lot of important questions that Dad would want to know the answers to, most of which David didn't know the answers to himself. After a while he started asking Garvey a few of them. He pretty much knew the answer to the first one, but he decided to ask anyway.

"Are we going to the Springer place?" he yelled.

"Yeah," Garvey yelled back. "That's where they keep them—the dogs—until this guy comes out from the city to pick them up in his truck."

David looked around. They were bouncing along a dirt road than ran between rows of apple trees. "Where are we? This isn't the way to the Springer place, is it?"

"Yeah, it is. This is the back way. It comes out on Murphy Road, on the other side of the property."

Okay, David thought. We're on our way to the Potters' stolen-dog hideout on a deserted old dairy farm, but don't ask me why. Maybe Nightmare is there and maybe he isn't. And is there any good reason to think that that's where the kids went? They could get there, all right, if they decided to do it. They knew which buses to take, and they probably had enough money in their piggy banks to pay the fares. But the big question is why would they go there? How would they have figured out that Nightmare might be there?

"You really think that's where the kids went?" he yelled at Garvey.

"Sure." Pete tended to turn partly around when he

answered questions, which took his eyes off the road. "Janie said she knew where Nightmare was, didn't she?" The bike hit a pothole and went into a skid. David grabbed Garvey around the middle and held on while they slid one way and then the other and finally regained their balance.

After a while, when David had stopped thinking of himself as another dirt bike accident statistic, he went back to Garvey's answer to his last question. Garvey, he thought, might very well be wrong. Contrary to popular opinion, Janie didn't always know what she was talking about. But he didn't tell Garvey that. In fact, the only thing he said for a long time was, "Keep your eyes on the road."

It wasn't until they slowed down and then came to a full stop on a wide shoulder that David began asking questions again. His first question was, "Where are we?"

Garvey was pulling the bike up a slope to a small acacia grove on a deserted stretch of country road. He shoved the bike in among the trees and then pointed toward the west. "We're almost there," he said. "That's part of the old Springer pasture, right there across the fence. We can sneak up to the barnyard along the creek bed."

"What are we going to do when we get there?"

Garvey grinned weakly. It was the first time David had seen him smile for a long time. "Hey, Davey," he said. "How come all the questions? I thought you were the dude with all the answers."

"Yeah." David grinned back. "Well, there are a few situations where I'm not exactly an authority. Like raiding the hideout of a bunch of dog-stealing thugs, for instance. But I'll try to come up with something. How about if we . . . sneak up the creek bed to the barn-yard?"

Garvey's chipped-toothed smile widened. "You got it," he said. "Let's go."

The creek, bordered by trees and bushes, wound across open pastureland for quite a long way. It wasn't until the land started to slope upward that there began to be any signs of civilization, if you could call it that. The first objects that came into view were the battered and rusty remains of cars and trucks. Scattered down the hillside as if they'd been thrown around by some angry giant, the dead and deader cars cluttered up the landscape all the way to the old Springer dairy build-ings.

David and Pete went on through the undergrowth along the creek bed until they reached a point from which there was a good view of the whole property. From behind the drooping limbs of a willow tree they looked out at an assortment of dilapidated paint-less dairy buildings surrounding an open area of hardpacked earth. A little farther away stood the old farmhouse, peeling and rickety. And everywhere there were more rusty cars and car parts.

"Do the Potters steal cars too?" David asked.

"Naw," Pete said. "Not whole cars, anyways. I guess they steal hubcaps and like that if they get a chance. But mostly they just pick up junkers for almost nothing and bring them here and strip them. They use some of the parts and sell some others and leave what's left lying around."

"And nobody cares about this mess? Do they live here alone? I mean, Normy and—what's the other guy's name?"

Pete grinned. "LeRoy. Normy and LeRoy Potter. You mean, do they have parents? Not exactly. Their ma lives here with them, but she doesn't pay any attention to what they do. Ma Potter probably gave up trying to tell Normy and LeRoy what to do when they were about five years old. She just—hey, look." Pete interrupted himself. "There's LeRoy now."

A tall wide-shouldered guy, maybe eighteen or nineteen years old, was coming down the back steps of the house. He had short spiky brown hair, and he was wearing a leather vest, oil-smeared jeans, and high black boots. Crossing the barnyard, he got something out of a pickup truck and went back inside.

"They're still here," Pete said. "I was hoping they'd have gone back to get the bikes by now. If all four of them were gone we could just go on up and look around. Ma Potter usually passes out by this time of day."

"So what'll we do now?"

"I dunno," Garvey said.

They sat under the willow tree a while longer trying to decide on their next move. The sun was getting low and the shadows around the buildings were deepening. It would soon be dark. There was no sign of the kids, or Nightmare. David was getting very antsy.

"Let's go on up to the barnyard and look around," he said.

"No," Pete said quickly. "That wouldn't be a good move."

"Well I'm getting tired of just sitting here. What if they have the kids inside the house? If the kids came on the bus they could have gotten here a long time ago. And those thugs could have them shut up somewhere. That's probably why they haven't gone back to get their dirt bikes: because they nabbed the kids and they're trying to decide what to do with them." David was standing up, and his voice was getting louder and louder. "Come on, Garvey. I want to find out. I want to go up and look in a window or something."

"Shhh!" Pete said. "You can't do that. They'll see you for sure, and then they'll just nab you too."

David sat down again. "Yeah, you're probably right."

After a minute Pete grabbed David's shoulder. "I got an idea. I'll go by myself. They know I already know about them stealing the dogs and all, and Ace told them I wouldn't rat on them or anything. So they won't care if I show up, as long as I'm alone. So I'll just—"

"Yeah," David said. "You could just say you went out to the lake to meet them and you found their bikes stashed there and came over here to find out what was going on."

Pete nodded. "Yeah. I'll go back and get the bike and ride on up to the house and say I just rode over to see why they went off and left their bikes. Then I can get in the house and look around. And you stay right here till I get back. Okay?"

"Okay," David said, and sat down to wait.

After only a few minutes he heard the faint faraway sound of the dirt bike's motor and he got up to watch it come up the hill. But nothing happened. No dirt bike and no Pete Garvey. What seemed like hours passed while David stood there straining his eyes in the fading light for a bike that didn't come.

I can't believe it, he told himself. Garvey must have chickened out and gone off by himself. He probably just went on home and forgot about the whole thing. That's what I get for trying to be friends with somebody like Pete Garvey.

Waiting there all alone under the willow tree while who knew what was going on in the ratty old farmhouse, David got more and more frantic. The whole thing—the gathering darkness, the dank smell of the creek bed, the senseless, hopeless waiting—all of it began to blur together like some kind of crazy endless nightmare. He had to do something. Anything. Anything was better than just sitting there. Peering out between the branches he began to plot a route up to the house.

He would have to leave the shelter of the creek bed and make his way up the open hillside. Out there the grass was only ankle deep, and there was no cover except for the scattering of broken-down cars. He would, he decided, dart from car to car like an Indian scout running from tree to tree. With his eyes on the house, where lights had come on in some of the windows, he made his first dash through the open and ducked behind the remains of a rusty station wagon. He waited there for a moment, his heart rattling against his ribs and his teeth clicking together like a drumroll. Then he got himself set again like a runner waiting for the starter's gun and took off.

His second stop was behind a VW bug. The wheelless blue body seemed to have sunk into the hillside, offering very little to hide behind, and David had to crouch low as he plotted his next advance. His next cover would be bigger and safer, the body of a large van that had once been painted white.

After again checking the house, for signs of activity, he gathered himself and sprinted up the hill. A few seconds later he was moving along behind the truck body to where he could peer out toward the house. He'd almost reached the corner when a deep echoing sound seemed to vibrate all around him. He jumped backward, tripped, and sat down in the grass. And the sound came again: "WOOF!" it went. "WOOF!"

He'd hardly hit the ground before he knew what it was. "Nightmare?" he whispered and the "WOOF!" came again, louder and more joyful, followed by a scratching noise, the sound of toenails on hard metal walls. So it was true. Nightmare *had* been stolen by the Potter gang, which might very well mean that Janie and the twins and the Tran kids were here, too—at least, if Janie was as good a detective as Pete seemed to think she was.

"Wow!" David whispered under his breath. He was glad to have found Nightmare, but he suddenly realized he was also a lot more frightened than he'd been before. His heart was beating harder than ever as he moved around the van looking for the doors. The walls were made of sturdy metal, and the double doors at the end were chained and padlocked. It took only a moment to be sure that there was no way he was going to break in, and no way that Nightmare, big and strong as he was, was going to break out. It looked pretty hopeless.

"Nightmare?" David said. "Shhh! Be quiet. I'll come back to get you as soon as I can. I have to go look for the kids."

"Woof," Nightmare said again, more softly.

"Good dog," David said, and got ready to make his next run up the hill.

A fancy Mercedes, which must have collided with a sixteen-wheeler, came next, and then a Ford Bronco with wheels but no tires or windshield. David was getting very close to the barnyard. Peering out from behind the Bronco, he cased the scene. Inside the house someone moved across a lighted window and then went back the way he'd come. A tall, heavyset guy, probably Mack or Normy. But the pickup was still sitting near the back porch and the barnyard was empty and deserted.

David checked the other buildings. The barn was closest, a huge ramshackle affair with a peaked roof and big double doors. The doors were open. David crept out from behind the broken-down Bronco and ran for it, right across the open yard, through the wide barn doors, and into darkness.

Inside the huge shadowy recess, evening turned immediately into night. Suddenly sightless, David slid to a quick stop and then froze, trying to make out the dim shadowy shapes that loomed around him. There were sounds, too—sounds were everywhere. Faint scrapes and rustles seemed to be coming from somewhere near his feet, and in the air all around him there were other noises. Hair-raising, throat-tightening noises: the leathery flutter and high-pitched squeaks of many small flying creatures.

David crouched low with his arms over his head. He didn't really have a phobia about bats. He just didn't like the idea of their getting into his hair or down his neck. Turning toward the door, he could see them against the light, flitting down from the loft and out and away into the twilight sky. Moving quickly to the side, to get out of the bats' flight path, he stumbled over a bale of hay and sat down hard.

"Ouch," a familiar voice said.

"Tesser?" David whispered.

"David," Esther whispered back. "Be careful. You sat on me."

Feeling frantically through a pile of loose hay, David's fingers felt a foot and then a leg. A short chubby leg. It was Esther, all right.

"Where's Janie?" David asked. "And the rest of the kids?"

Something rustled a little farther away, and Janie said, "I'm over here." The rustle got louder. "We were all hiding," she said. "We all made hiding places in the hay before it got so dark. And then we heard running and we didn't know who it was, so we dove for cover. You can come out now. It's just David."

The rustling noises got louder, and in a minute he could see them—just barely see them—all around him. All three, four, five of them. Four small shadowy figures, and one even smaller.

David let all the exasperation of the last couple of hours into his voice. "Janie, what are you *doing* here?"

"I told you," Janie whispered. "In the note. I told you I deduced that the hot-rod guys had stolen Nightmare.

And we knew they lived here. So we came here to get him."

"But why did you sneak out like that? Why didn't you wake me up and tell me you were going?"

"Because you wouldn't have let us," Janie said, which David had to admit was probably the truth.

"We had to come get Nightmare," another voice came out of the darkness.

"Blair?" David said.

"Yes. We had to, David. Those car guys stole Nightmare, so we had to come get him. David, did you see him? Do you know where Nightmare is?"

"Yes, I know. I know where he is but—"

"Where?" Blair was grabbing David's arm, shaking it. "Where is he?"

"He's just a little way down the hill, shut up in a big white van. But it's locked, and I couldn't get in. We'll have to get the key or a crowbar or something to force the lock with. We'll have to—Blair? Where are you?"

The sound of running feet made David whirl around just in time to see Blair running out through the open doors of the barn.

"Blair!" David ran after him calling as loudly as he dared. "Blair. Come back here."

But Blair didn't stop. By the time David caught up with him he had reached the stairs that led up to the back door of the farmhouse. Grabbing him by the back of his jacket, David pulled him off the steps and onto the ground.

"Where do you think you're going?" he whispered. "You can't go in there!"

"I'm going to get the key. I'm going to ask them for the key to the place where Nightmare is."

"No you're not. They won't give it to you. They won't—"

Just at that moment a yard light came on, the door of the farmhouse banged open, and one of the Potters appeared at the top of the stairs. The others were right behind him, all three of them. As David backed away pulling Blair after him, Ace and Mack and the two Potters followed, their boots thudding noisily on the wooden steps.

David had only backed a few steps when he bumped into someone and realized that the other kids had followed him out of the barn. Now all five of them were clustered around him.

"Well, would ya look at this," one of the Potters said. "Look who we got here. Snow White and all them dwarfs." He moved forward in a half crouch, spreading his arms. "Scatter out, men, let's catch us some dwarfs."

As David and the kids went on backing away, the four guys spread out around them and moved forward. David put up his fists. "Stay back," he said. "Don't come any closer."

They all laughed and kept coming, and they laughed even harder when Blair suddenly said, "You better not hurt us. The policemen are coming."

"Sure they are, kid," Mack Maillard said. "Where have I heard that one before?"

"Here they come," Blair said, and it was just a few seconds later that a black and white police car roared down the driveway.

Conclusion

"And at that very moment," Janie said, "Officer Donnelly and the other policeman drove right down the driveway and arrested the dognappers. And then Officer Donnelly called on his radio for another police car to take the dognappers to jail, and David showed him where Nightmare was, and he got Nightmare out of the van, and then we all came back here in the police car. The end." Janie made a little bow and said, "The end," again and everybody applauded. All the police officers clapped and cheered and so did the twins and the Tran kids. And even Nightmare, who was lying on the floor beside Officer Donnelly's desk, wagged his tail and barked once or twice. David applauded too, even though he couldn't help noticing that there had been a few gaps in Janie's version of the case of the Steven's Corners dognappers.

Janie's version, of course, had been full of stuff about

the Jane Victoria Stanley Agency and how they had been working on the stolen dog mystery so that the Tran kids' father wouldn't lose his job. When she got to that part she'd introduced Thuy and Huy to everyone, and some of the women officers made a big fuss over how cute they were.

She also went into the Mayor Sam investigation, which most of the officers seemed to remember from the Stanleys' previous visit to the police station.

"I made a mistake about that," she said, "because I hadn't deduced yet that the dognappers were only stealing fancy pedigreed dogs. Like they weren't interested in any ugly old mutts like Mayor Sam."

Yeah, David thought. That's right. I should have noticed that.

After that she'd gone on about how she'd deduced this and that and the other thing, including that the Potters were the thieves. She'd deduced that, she said, because they'd been riding their dirt bikes in the hills when Nightmare had disappeared—which was pretty circumstantial evidence, if anybody had been noticing. But nobody seemed to be, except for David. And nobody asked him for his opinion.

David had been asked a few questions a little earlier. In fact, he'd gotten to ride back from the Springer place in the front seat of the patrol car, and on the way Officer Donnelly had asked him about a lot of details.

As it happened, one of the questions Officer Donnelly asked him cleared up a very important detail that had been bothering him a lot: how the police had happened to show up at the Springer place just in the nick of time. He'd gotten the answer to that one when Officer Donnelly asked, "Who called the station about what was going on out there? The guy that took the call said it sounded like a kid, some very excited-sounding kid who said the Potters and the Maillards were involved in the dog thefts, and that someone was in big trouble out at the old Springer dairy. Was it you that called?"

"No," David said. "It wasn't. I don't know who it was."

It wasn't a lie, either, because it wasn't until he thought about it a minute that it occurred to him who it must have been. It had to have been Garvey. Garvey must have called the police after he left the Springer place. He'd called the police and ratted on the Potters, but he hadn't given the police his name.

Okay, David thought, I won't bring him into it either. Not unless I have to. And since nobody asked any more questions about the phone call, he didn't have to. He answered the rest of Officer Donnelly's questions completely, except for one where he had to fudge a little, because of trying not to mention Pete Garvey. That was the one about how he had known that the little kids had gone to the Springer place. "Janie left a note," he said, which, of course, was true; the only fudging part was the minor detail that the note hadn't said where they were going.

So David didn't tell about what Garvey had done, and of course neither did Janie, since she didn't know he was involved at all. But Janie answered every other question anybody asked her, and a lot more no one even thought of asking, and about the time she was finished Dad and Molly rushed into the police station and it was all over. At least, it was all over for that night, but the next day was something else.

The whole next week, in fact, was fairly exciting, especially for Janie. In the first place, Dad let her off easy for going on with her investigations after he'd shut down her detective agency. Right at first he did blast her a little, of course, but he forgave her pretty quickly. He almost had to, because she was getting so much publicity and attention for what she'd done.

After the Maillards and the Potters confessed, the police tracked down the guy in the city who'd been buying the stolen dogs. Most of the missing dogs were located and returned to their owners, including the McGarritys' Lad and Mrs. Ferris's Phoebe. In fact, just about the only dog that the police weren't able to find any trace of was the Boggses' Doberman, Rambo.

Several of the owners called up to thank Janie and the kids for what they had done, and the McGarritys insisted on giving the Jane Victoria Stanley Agency the reward money they had offered for Highland Lad. So each of the kids got one hundred dollars, which Janie was really excited about, until she found out that Dad was going to make her and the twins put most of it in their college education accounts at the bank.

Then a couple of days later a strange thing happened. A man who lived way out in the country called up the Steven's Corners police and told them he'd read about the dog thefts in the paper and thought he knew where Rambo was. Somebody, he said, had dumped a big friendly Doberman near his ranch, on the very night that Rambo was supposedly stolen. David found out about it when he read the police report in the *Valley Press*, and it got him thinking.

Some of the things he thought about were 1. that Billy Boggs had been the one who started a lot of the schoolyard rumors about the Trans being the dog thieves, and 2. that Mr. Boggs owned a company that built shopping centers, and the offer for Mr. Wright's nursery had come from someone who'd wanted the land to build a shopping center on. Number 3. Rambo was about the fourth dog to disappear—as if the first few might have given someone the idea of getting rid of a dog he didn't much like and at the same time adding to the rumors against the Trans.

So David called up Mr. Wright and asked him the name of the company that wanted to buy the nursery land. At first Mr. Wright, who had always been kind of grumpy, wasn't going to tell him.

"What business is it of yours, young man?" he said.

But finally he started listening, and David told him some of the things he'd been thinking about. Mr. Wright was quiet for a long time, and then he started muttering in an angry-sounding voice and hung up the phone without even saying good-bye. But about an hour later he called back and said that Boggs and Turner was the company who wanted his land. And he also said he'd been asking around town and he'd discovered that Boggs and his partner had done a lot of rumor-spreading about the Trans and the dog thefts.

"Guess he thought if I lost Tran I'd give up on keeping the nursery running, and I almost did, too," he told David.

"So you're not going to sell after all?" David asked,

and Mr. Wright said, "No siree, not on your tintype!" and some other comments like that and hung up again without saying good-bye. And the next day Thuy called Janie and said that Mr. Wright had told her father that he wasn't going to sell the nursery after all, and the job was his as long as he wanted it. And that night Molly had a celebration dinner for the Trans and cooked a salmon soufflé and a bunch of other fancy stuff without burning anything.

So a lot of people had something to celebrate, including David, who finally got his newspaper article finished. On the day after the Potters and Maillards were arrested, Garvey called up and then came over and they got everything straightened out. Garvey said he'd really intended to do what he said he would when he left David under the willow tree: he intended to ride up to the farmhouse and see what he could find out. But on the way down to the bike he'd decided that what he had to do was call the police. "Sometimes you got to do what's right," he said, "even if it's ratting on guys you thought were your friends."

And David agreed with him. In fact, David said a lot about what a brilliant decision he'd made and what a lot of credit he deserved for making it.

But Pete didn't want any credit. What he did want, though, was back in on the newspaper project. So they went back to work on the final write-up, and Garvey went back to being in love with Amanda, and Amanda went back to treating him like dirt, and everybody was more or less happy again.

David felt pretty good too. And so did Mr. Edmonds

when they turned in the Stanley-Garvey news story. Mr. Edmonds really liked the story. He said it was a great example of the importance of good investigative reporting, but he did make David change the ending a little before it was printed in the *Valley Press.*

"Keep your own feelings out of it," Mr. Edmonds said. "Just put in what you have proof of. Just give us the facts."

So David took out the part about what a creep he thought Mr. Boggs was, and the story was printed in the *Valley Press.* And Mr. Edmonds was right. The facts were enough, because right afterward business began to pick up a lot at the nursery and the Boggs family moved out of town.

Nobody ever seemed to notice that there were a couple of *missing* facts in the Stanley-Garvey news article. Missing explanations like who called the police, which David knew but wasn't telling, and how the little kids had figured out that the Potters were the dog thieves, which he still wasn't sure about. Most people just don't think about details like that, David decided. David himself had pretty much stopped thinking about them, until one Saturday when he happened to see a picture that Esther was drawing.

Esther was drawing the picture in the dining room when David came in to do some homework. She had a big piece of paper spread out on the table, and she was kneeling on a chair so she could reach it better. Her tongue was sticking out of the corner of her mouth, and she was concentrating so hard she didn't even notice David until he came over to see what she was doing.

"What's all this?" he asked.

"See, that's the driveway," she said, pointing to two long lines that went clear across the paper. "And over here is Blair, and on this side, this is me and that's Janie and Thuy and Huy. See, we're just going down the driveway to the bus stop to go out and rescue Nightmare from the dognappers."

David checked out the picture. "Why is Blair way over here by himself?"

"Because he went first. He told us that he was going to that place where the cows used to live to get Nightmare and then he left and we had to hurry to catch up. See, here we are, hurrying."

"You mean it was Blair who figured out where they'd taken Nightmare?"

Esther put her hand over her mouth and her eyes got rounder. "Ohhh. I wasn't supposed to say that."

"Tesser!" David said. "What do you mean you weren't supposed to say that?"

"I was supposed to say that Janie deduced it."

"And it was really Blair who deduced it?"

"Deduced? Well, what Blair said was . . . that he just knew it. All of a sudden he just knew it. You know. Blair knows things sometimes."

"Yeah," David said. "I've heard some rumors to that effect."

Esther was looking worried. "I wasn't supposed to tell. Blair says knowing things can get you into trouble. Are you going to tell on him?"

David sat down at the table and opened his book and thought for a minute. Then he grinned at Esther. "We wouldn't want to get anybody in trouble for something like that, would we?"

Esther shook her head hard. Then she went back to drawing the picture of Blair running down the drive-way way ahead of everybody else.

About the Author

Zilpha Keatley Snyder is the author of three other books that feature the adventurous Stanley family: *The Headless Cupid* (a Newbery Honor book), *The Famous Stanley Kidnapping Case,* and *Blair's Nightmare.* Her stories *The Witches of Worm* and *The Egypt Game* were also named Newbery Honor books. Her most recent books are *And Condors Danced* and *Squeak Saves the Day.*

Zilpha Keatley Snyder lives with her husband in Marin County, California.